Mail Order Mayor
Book 56 in Brides of Be
Kirsten Osbourne

Copyright © 2024 by Kirsten Osbourne

Unlimited Dreams Publishing

All rights reserved.

Cover design by Erin Dameron Hill/ EDH Graphics

No part of this book may be reproduced in any form or by any electronic or mechanical means including information storage and retrieval systems, without permission in writing from the author. The only exception is by a reviewer, who may quote short excerpts in a review.

This book is a work of fiction. Names, characters, places, and incidents either are products of the author's imagination or are used fictitiously. Any resemblance to actual persons, living or dead, events, or locales is entirely coincidental.

Kirsten Osbourne

Visit my website at www.kirstenandmorganna.com

Chapter One

Amy Brown's day started much too early, her feet padding softly across the cold wooden floors of the foundling home where she'd been raised. With tender hands and a gentle hum, she roused the slumbering orphans, her "sisters" of circumstance rather than blood. A smile graced her lips as sleepy eyes blinked up at her.

"Up you get," Amy whispered, tucking stray locks behind tiny ears and straightening tousled nightgowns. Her heart swelled with every giggle and yawn, every small hand that found hers in the dim morning light. Though not a mother by name, she was one in every other sense to these girls, and she held onto the hope that one day she would extend such love to children of her own.

Meanwhile, some two thousand miles away, Timothy Stockwell stood against the vast backdrop of his Fort Worth ranch. He loved his life and the work he did, but since his wife had died, everything was harder. He watched his herd, but his thoughts were with the chaos brewing back at the house.

"Pa, I can't find my boots!" George's voice called out.

"Beatrice, have you seen your brother's boots?" Tim called out, knowing the futility even before the words left his mouth.

"No, and I don't care! I'm not the maid," came the sullen reply from his twelve-year-old daughter.

Tim sighed. He loved this land, but without his beloved Felicity, the house no longer felt like a home. It was a structure that kept the rain off him and his four children.

AMY FINISHED TYING the littlest one's shoes, her gaze drifting toward the window. She allowed herself a short moment to dream of wide-open spaces and the laughter of children that were truly hers. Her mind painted a picture of a life far removed from the institutional walls of the foundling home—a life filled with love, joy, and the bustling activity of a family she could call her own.

Not that she had ever felt unloved at the foundling home. The matron had hidden her there for a while before there had been a spot for her to work there. Most girls in her position ended up as factory workers, maids, or nannies. She had no desire to be any of those things. She was intelligent enough to know what she wanted from life, and what she wanted was a family of her own.

TIMOTHY WIPED THE SWEAT from his brow as he returned to the house, the aroma of an attempted breakfast wafting out to greet him. His attempts at cooking had not been successful, and he longed for the delicate flavors and loving preparations his wife used to make. As he faced another day of makeshift meals and mounting chores, he couldn't shake the feeling that something needed to change. Not just for his sake, but for the children, each one as lost in this new world as he was.

But whether Felicity was there or not, he was their father, and it was his job to raise them, and that meant sending them to school with full stomachs.

AMY TIED HER APRON strings in a neat bow at her back, ready to face the day's chores. The kitchen of the foundling home was her domain, and it was her task to teach the girls to cook. She loved to teach the girls, just as she'd been taught by the older girls when she was younger.

Her cheeks flushed with the warmth of the oven, Amy hummed her favorite hymn while she whisked eggs for breakfast, envisioning a bustling kitchen filled with her own brood. She couldn't get the thought of having children out of her mind that day—or any other day for that matter.

"Amy," piped up a small voice, interrupting her thoughts, "how do you know if someone will ever love you?"

Amy turned to see little Susie, one of her nine charges, clutching a rag doll and looking up with wide-eyed innocence. She knelt. "Oh, "she spoke gently, "love has a way of finding us when we least expect it."

With breakfast served and the clatter of spoons against bowls filling the air, Amy busied herself with the day's cleaning. Each sweep was a step closer to her imagined future, each polished surface reflecting her hope for a chance at love.

The afternoon brought mending. The orphans' clothes were well-loved and often in need of repair. Amy threaded her needle with practiced ease. The children gathered around, their conversations weaving through the fabric of her thoughts.

"Miss Amy, can you make my dress pretty like yours?" asked Daisy, her eyes following the needle's dance.

"Every stitch I make is meant to make you feel special," Amy replied.

In the quiet moments, between the guidance she offered and the laughter she shared, Amy held fast to the belief that somewhere beyond these walls, love awaited—a love that would grant her the family she yearned for and transform her dreams into reality.

Amy paused as she worked on fixing a little one's trousers. A daydream took hold as she peered outside, watching the cottonwood seeds flutter in the breeze. She imagined herself not as an orphan but as a mother, surrounded by children of her own, each with bright eyes and laughter. For a fleeting moment, Amy wondered about the woman who had left her wrapped in swaddling at the foundling home's doorstep—did she ever peer out of a window, dreaming of the daughter she could not keep?

TWO THOUSAND MILES away in Fort Worth, Timothy Stockwell was wrestling with a pot over the stove, the contents bubbling and protesting as he attempted to coax supper from its depths. His brow furrowed; his wife had made it look so easy.

"Beatrice, can you fetch the plates?" he called out.

"No," came the sullen reply from the doorway. Beatrice clutched her arms, a scowl etching her young features. "Mama should be doing that, not me."

"Your ma would've wanted us to stick together, Bea," Tim said, his voice gentle yet tinged with the fatigue of many such conversations.

But Beatrice turned sharply, leaving Tim to navigate fatherhood alone, his heart aching for a companion's touch in the middle of the chaos of his love-filled but unruly home.

TIM WIPED THE SWEAT from his brow as he hoisted another bale of hay onto the wagon under the relentless Texas sun. As he secured the hay, his thoughts wandered to the chaos of last night's dinner, the children's squabbles, and the untamed laundry pile mocking him.

"Lord knows, I need help," he muttered under his breath, a half-prayer, half-plea to the open sky. The idea of remarrying twisted inside him like a lasso. It wasn't just about love; it was survival, structure...sanity.

A shadow fell across the pasture, and Timothy recognized Beatrice's slender frame approaching. Her steps were heavy, burdened with grief. Her eyes, once bright as Texas Bluebonnets, now were filled with a sorrow that wouldn't go away.

"Pa, why do we still keep Mama's garden?"

Timothy set down the pitchfork and walked over to her. "Your mama loved that garden," he said softly. "Keeping it alive feels right, like she's still with us."

Beatrice's arms folded tightly against her chest, her lips pressed into a thin line. "But she's not," she snapped. "And no one else can pretend to be her, either."

"Never," Tim promised, his own heart constricting. "No one could ever take your mama's place." He reached out, hoping she would lean into the offered embrace.

But Beatrice stepped back. "Just leave me alone," she whispered before turning on her heel and walking back toward the house, leaving Timothy alone once more with his thoughts.

As he watched her retreat, the weight of solitude settled on his shoulders. Maybe, just maybe, there was someone out there who could bring a new kind of love to their home.

TIM STOOD IN THE FIELD, his son beside him. George manned the plow with youthful zeal, his lean muscles already taking on the definition of a rancher's life.

"Pa," George said, pausing to catch his breath, "I've been thinking."

"About?" Timothy asked, offering the boy a swig from his canteen.

"About land. Someday, I want a piece of this earth too, just over yonder." He gestured broadly to the horizon. "Close enough so we can work together every day."

Timothy smiled at the thought. "I would like that a great deal, son."

"Me too!" George exclaimed, his eyes alight with future dreams.

AS EVENING FELL, AMY gathered the orphans in the common room of Brown's Foundling Home. The smell of freshly baked bread still lingered in the air, a testament to her day's work. She sat down in the oversized armchair, the fabric worn smooth by years of use.

"Miss Amy, I want to sit with you!" little Sarah called out.

"Me first! Miss Amy promised yesterday!" Peter interjected, trying to climb onto her lap before anyone else.

"Children, there's enough of me to go around," Amy chuckled, her heart full. With practiced ease, she settled one child on each knee and began to read from a book of fairy tales, her voice lulling them into a world where every story promised a happy ending.

AMY NESTLED INTO THE makeshift bed on the floor, a quilt folded beneath her for cushioning. She was too old to sleep among the girls there, yet this foundling home was all she knew. Her eyes traced the gentle rise and fall of each sleeping form, these sisters of circumstance, before closing her own.

"Goodnight," she whispered to the room, though none stirred at her words.

As sleep claimed her, Amy imagined a cozy farmhouse, its windows aglow with the warmth of a family inside. Laughter repeated from within its walls, and the scent of vanilla and cinnamon wafted out as the front door opened.

In her dream, Amy stood in the kitchen, rolling dough with flour-covered hands. Children's giggles filled the air, and she turned to see her children. They tumbled around the wooden floors, their cheeks rosy from play.

"Supper will be ready soon!" she called out.

Outside, beyond the picket fence, stretched fields of golden crops, and a man—strong, kind, her partner in every way—waved from where he repaired a fence post.

"Mama, tell us a story!" a little one pleaded, tugging at the hem of her skirt in the dream.

"All right, my sweet," Amy agreed, lifting the child into her lap. "Once upon a time…"

The words flowed naturally, a tale spun from hope and heart, while in the real world, Amy's breaths deepened as she settled into the most perfect dream in the world. The dream of a man who loved her and at least a dozen children.

TIM SHIFTED UNEASILY in the hard wooden pew, his gaze fixed on the stained glass window as the pastor's voice repeated through the small chapel. Beside him, David Dailey, a fellow rancher and friend, leaned closer.

"Something on your mind, Tim?" David whispered, his eyebrows lifting in concern beneath the brim of his Sunday hat.

Tim nodded, glancing toward where his eldest daughter, Beatrice, sat with her chin defiantly tilted upwards, her expression stormy. "Beatrice," he murmured, the name heavy with worry. "She's been…well, she's been downright rude since her ma passed. I can hardly keep up."

David gave a sympathetic nod. "Kids'll test you at every turn, especially when they're hurting. But you've got four to wrangle on top of running that big ranch of yours."

"Exactly." Tim ran a hand through his hair. "I'm out there from sunup till sundown, trying to keep things together. When I come back to the house, it's like stepping into a hornet's nest. And supper..." He shook his head. "Let's just say we've had beans from a can more times this week than I care to admit."

"Sounds like you need help, my friend," David said with a chuckle. The man had mastered the art of seeming to pay rapt attention to the pastor while conversing about something different entirely.

"Help would be a blessing," Tim agreed. "But where do you find someone willing to step into this mess? Someone who can handle the ranch life and...well, and Beatrice."

"Patience and love, Tim. That's what they need," David advised, patting Tim's shoulder reassuringly. "And you need a touch of stubbornness to match your daughter's."

"Seems like I'm asking for a miracle," Tim sighed, half-joking.

"Miracles happen, especially in these parts," David replied with a wink. "Keep your chin up, Tim. Things have a way of working themselves out."

The preacher's final "Amen" released the congregation, and as the chapel emptied, Tim felt a sliver of hope. Maybe David was right; maybe there was someone out there who could bring warmth and laughter back into their home. With a prayer tucked away in his chest, Timothy Stockwell stepped out into the bright Texas sun, ready to face another week on his beloved ranch, children, and all.

Chapter Two

Elizabeth Tandy pushed open the weathered door of Brown's Foundling Home. Tied back in a loose bun, her blond hair glinted gold in the sunlight. The green of her eyes mirrored the hope she carried for the girls who resided within these walls.

"Good afternoon!" Elizabeth greeted. She brushed off her skirts, stepping further inside.

Mrs. Jackson, the matron who had watched over Amy and the other children, descended the stairs to meet her visitor. "And who do I have the pleasure of meeting?" she asked, her gaze appraising the well-dressed woman before her.

"Elizabeth Tandy," she said, extending a hand. "I'm a matchmaker from Beckham. I've come with an offer that might interest you and your girls."

"A matchmaker, you say?" Mrs. Jackson's brows lifted in curiosity as she led Elizabeth into a modest parlor. "Please, have a seat. How can you help our young women?"

"What I do is match young women up with men in the west to marry. They exchange letters, or sometimes simply one letter and a telegram, and they are off to marry. I've been doing this for many years now, and I've not matched people who didn't eventually fall in love. Some take longer than others, but they all get there in the end. The men pay for the women's fares to the west, so the girls don't need to worry with that expense."

"These girls are like my own children," Mrs. Jackson admitted, taking a chair opposite her guest. "I don't like the idea of any of them marrying someone sight unseen. I just don't think it's safe."

Elizabeth folded her hands neatly in her lap. "I find respectable men looking for wives and arrange for them to meet women looking for husbands. It's about finding compatibility, giving both a chance to choose."

"Compatibility..." Mrs. Jackson mused. "That sounds reasonable. But these girls, they're not just names on a list to me. They're unique, each with dreams and desires."

"Of course," Elizabeth assured her, her tone earnest. "It's not just about marriage—it's about creating happy homes. It's a chance for new beginnings. I've sent many of my siblings to marry people in the west."

"New beginnings," Mrs. Jackson repeated softly. "That's all any mother wants for her children, isn't it?"

"Exactly," Elizabeth replied, a warm smile spreading across her face. "Together, we can give them that chance."

Through a crack in the kitchen door, Amy's gaze lingered on the two women conversing in the parlor. The words 'new beginnings' and 'chance for love' wafted through the air. A spark ignited in Amy's chest—a flicker of hope that danced in her eyes.

"Marriage..." she whispered to herself. Her heart raced at the thought, her hands pausing while kneading dough.

"Mrs. Tandy?" Amy's voice quivered slightly as she stepped into the room, her apron dusted with flour. She tucked a loose strand of chestnut hair behind her ear, her posture straightening with resolve.

Elizabeth turned toward her, a question in her green eyes. "Yes, my dear?"

"Um..." A brief hesitation, then Amy's conviction solidified. "I overheard talk of...matchmaking?"

"That's right." Elizabeth's voice was gentle, inviting.

"Could I...Would it be possible for me to find someone? To have a real family?" Amy asked.

"Oh, my," Elizabeth replied, tilting her head, considering the young woman before her. "You wish for a husband, then?"

"Yes, ma'am," Amy nodded eagerly. "A home...children." Her cheeks colored with the admission, but she held Elizabeth's gaze firmly. "Lots of them."

"Children are such a blessing," Elizabeth agreed with a soft laugh. "And you cook, I take it?"

"Best pies in Cheerful," Amy said with a hint of pride.

"Then we shall see what can be done, Amy. We'll find you a man who appreciates a good pie as much as a good wife," Elizabeth promised.

"Thank you, Mrs. Tandy. Thank you so much!" Amy's face was filled with gratitude. "I'll have to give notice, of course, so I can come see you in two weeks. Would you mind sharing your address with me?"

Elizabeth shook her head, laughing. "Of course not. I'll write down my address for you, and you can come any time." She took the pencil and paper offered by Mrs. Jackson and quickly scrawled her address.

Amy's heart swelled. She clutched her hands together, the promise of a future painted in her thoughts.

"Thank you, Mrs. Tandy," Amy breathed out, relief and excitement mingling in her words.

"Call me Elizabeth," the matchmaker corrected kindly, her tone suggesting the closeness of friends rather than the formality of their current acquaintance.

"Elizabeth," Amy repeated.

From across the room, Mrs. Jackson watched the exchange, her brows knitting together in a frown of concern. She took slow, measured steps toward them, her skirts whispering against the polished wooden floor.

"Matchmaking is fine talk," Mrs. Jackson interjected, her voice careful but firm. "But these girls are like my own." She glanced at Amy, the bond between them as visible as the lines of worry etching her brow. "I fear for them, out there with strangers."

"Mrs. Jackson," Elizabeth said. "I understand your fears. But I assure you, we're talking about honest men, looking for companionship just as much as these young women are."

"Men can be unpredictable," Mrs. Jackson countered, folding her arms. "And words sweet as honey can turn bitter."

"Which is why they'll be investigated first. If I can't get quick answers to telegrams asking about the men, then I send my husband, Bernard, to check on them. No one's rushing to the altar," Elizabeth explained, her patience evident.

"Still," Mrs. Jackson hesitated. "It's a big world outside this home."

"Sometimes," Elizabeth said, "a leap of faith is all it takes to find where we belong."

"Faith," Mrs. Jackson murmured, the word hanging between them like a prayer.

"Exactly," Elizabeth nodded, reassuringly. "We'll take care of our girls, won't we?"

Mrs. Jackson's gaze lingered on Amy, the oldest of her charges, who stood with eyes full of dreams. "Let me think on it, and I'll come talk to you."

Amy lingered by the doorway, apron dusted with flour from the morning's bread-making. She took a deep breath and approached Mrs. Jackson who was tidying the modest parlor.

"Mrs. Jackson?" Amy's voice was gentle but determined. "May I speak with you?"

The matron paused, setting aside a pile of mending. "Of course, dear," she said, her eyes softening at the sight of Amy's earnest face.

"I've been thinking about what Mrs. Tandy said." Amy clasped her hands together, her gaze steady. "About finding a family…"

Mrs. Jackson nodded, encouraging her to continue.

"This place, it's been more than a home. It's been a family, thanks to you." Amy's eyes traced the familiar walls. "I've watched over the girls like they were my sisters. But I have dreams, Mrs. Jackson. Dreams of a husband, a house filled with laughter and children—a dozen of them."

A smile tugged at the corners of Mrs. Jackson's mouth. "A dozen is quite the handful," she said.

"Yes, but full hands mean a full heart," Amy replied.

Mrs. Jackson studied Amy for a long moment, the weight of years spent nurturing these young souls pressing upon her. Then, slowly, she reached out and took Amy's hands in hers. "You do deserve that full heart, child. And love...love beyond these walls. But the idea of letting you go causes me so much pain."

Tears welled in Amy's eyes, reflecting the shimmer in Mrs. Jackson's own. "I'll never forget this place or you. You've given me so much, taught me how to be kind and helpful. I want to share that with a family of my own."

Mrs. Jackson pulled Amy into an embrace, her resolve strengthening. "Then we shall make sure of it," she whispered, her voice thick with emotion. "We'll find you that family, my dear. A family where your kindness can bloom and your dreams can soar."

"Thank you," Amy murmured, feeling the depth of the bond they shared, one not even distance could sever.

"Let's have faith," Mrs. Jackson said as they parted, a tear escaping down her cheek. "Faith that there's a perfect match for you out there."

MRS. JACKSON SQUARED her shoulders and took a deep breath before rapping on the polished wooden door of Elizabeth Tandy's residence. Her heart felt light as the door swung open, revealing the matchmaker's bright green eyes and welcoming smile.

"Mrs. Jackson! What a pleasant surprise," Elizabeth exclaimed, stepping aside to allow the matron inside her home. "We'll go to the last door on the left." She called out, "Bernard!" and at once a tall man with blond hair and eyes came to her. "Mrs. Jackson and I would like tea and cookies, if you don't mind."

Bernard gave one nod. "Absolutely."

"Thank you, Elizabeth. I hope I'm not intruding," Mrs. Jackson began as Elizabeth waved to indicate she should sit. She settled onto a sofa, the scent of fresh-baked bread wafting from the kitchen.

"Never," Elizabeth assured her, taking a seat opposite her guest. "What brings you here today?"

"It's about the girls," Mrs. Jackson said, hands clasped in her lap. "I have nine young women who are of age to marry. They're ready to head west, to begin lives of their own."

Elizabeth nodded, her expression turning thoughtful. "How wonderful. Though I'm sure you'll miss them."

"However," continued Mrs. Jackson, "I can't bear the thought of sending them off as mail-order brides, marrying men they've never laid eyes on."

A soft frown creased Elizabeth's forehead. "I understand your concern. Sight unseen does seem quite precarious. And even though I've seen it happen myself over fifty times, doesn't mean that you will trust me or the men on the other side of the mail system."

"Exactly," Mrs. Jackson said. "And truth be told, I haven't been asking the girls to move on when they come of age. The home is crowded, but..." She sighed, her gaze falling to the well-worn carpet. "They sleep wherever there's place. It's become a bit of a jumble, but they're my girls."

Elizabeth reached across and gently touched Mrs. Jackson's hand. "I admire your dedication to them," she said warmly. "You've given them a family within those walls."

"Thank you." A small smile tugged at Mrs. Jackson's lips. "But it's time they had families outside of them too."

"That's true," Elizabeth agreed. "And we'll find a way to help them do just that."

Elizabeth paced the parlor slowly. She paused and turned to face Mrs. Jackson with a sudden burst of inspiration.

"Mrs. Jackson, I believe I have a plan!" Elizabeth exclaimed, her voice tinged with excitement. "I will write to my sisters in Texas. They can help find respectable men who are looking for wives. We'll arrange for a social gathering—a party at their church. They have social gatherings there at least once a month, so no one will mind."

Mrs. Jackson's brow furrowed slightly, skepticism mingling with her concern. "A party, you say?"

"Yes," Elizabeth continued with a reassuring nod. "It will be a proper occasion. We'll ensure there is a pastor present, should any matches be made. It's much better than just exchanging letters, don't you think? The girls can meet these gentlemen in person—and what's more, I will personally meet them."

The matron of the orphanage took a moment to consider this unconventional idea. Her protective instincts warred with the opportunity for her girls to find love and happiness.

"Elizabeth, I must admit, your plan has merit," Mrs. Jackson finally said, her voice steady but cautious. "But I insist on accompanying the girls myself. I need to see with my own eyes that they will be well-matched and cared for."

"Of course, I wouldn't have it any other way," Elizabeth replied. "Together, we will watch over them during this journey, and I shall have the opportunity to visit my sisters."

"Very well," Mrs. Jackson agreed, her resolve strengthening with the thought of embarking on such an adventure for the sake of the girls she held so dear. "We shall take great care in guiding them toward their futures."

Elizabeth said, "It seems the stars have aligned perfectly for us. My children are now old enough that I can leave them in my husband's care for a few weeks. It's an opportune moment for me to visit Susan and her family, as well as Alice and her husband, in Fort Worth."

Mrs. Jackson nodded, her eyes reflecting the hope that was slowly replacing her initial apprehension. "That sounds like a sensible plan, Elizabeth. I'm sure your sisters will be delighted to have you."

Without further delay, Elizabeth retrieved a sheet of stationery and a well-worn fountain pen from her desk. She settled herself by the window, allowing the afternoon light to guide her hand as she penned a heartfelt letter to her sister. The words flowed effortlessly, filled with the news of their impending visit and the unique purpose behind it.

TWO WEEKS LATER, A response arrived, bearing the familiar scrawl of Susan Dailey. Elizabeth eagerly broke the seal and unfolded the letter, her green eyes scanning the lines hungrily.

"Dearest Elizabeth," Susan had written, "nothing could excite me more than the prospect of your visit! You and Mrs. Jackson shall have the coziest rooms in our home, and we'll find a way to accommodate the girls as well. Fort Worth will welcome you with open arms!"

Elizabeth called to her husband. "We need to go to Brown's Foundling Home!"

Bernard walked to her. "I'm happy to drive you. Did you receive the letter?"

Bernard had started out as Elizabeth's butler and her investigator of grooms. As they'd married, he'd chosen to keep doing the same tasks he'd done before marriage, and it had worked out well for both of them.

Elizabeth checked on the children, who were with their nanny, Angela, a former resident of the orphanage there in Beckham. "Are they all right?" she asked.

Angela nodded. "Yes, Mrs. Tandy. They're perfect."

"Bernard and I need to drive to the foundling home in Cheerful. We shouldn't be long."

Angela smiled. "Take your time and enjoy the drive. Go out for supper. I don't mind working this evening."

Elizabeth grinned. "We'd like that. Thank you!" As she walked down the stairs, she made a mental note to pay the girl for an extra day that week.

In the buggy, Elizabeth told Bernard about how enthusiastic Susan had sounded about her visit. "Are you sure you don't mind staying with the children?" she asked.

Bernard laughed. "Even if I did, I would tell you to go. You need some time with Susan. And if I run into any trouble, I have Angela, Mary, and your parents close by."

"That's true. Oh, thank you for letting me do this. I'll help the girls and receive a much-needed vacation from my normal duties."

Bernard wrapped his arm around her shoulders. "I'm glad you'll get the reprieve."

"Speaking of reprieves...Angela said we should go out for supper. Do you think Boston is too far away?"

Bernard laughed. "The children aren't that unruly."

"Which children do you live with?" Elizabeth asked. Their children weren't truly unruly. It was more they were young and boisterous. They weren't doing as Elizabeth's younger siblings had and hanging upside down from trees over the road as they threw rotten vegetables.

He chuckled. "I would love to take you for supper. There's a new restaurant near the general store. They are purported to have exceptional food."

"Purported," Elizabeth said, shaking her head. "You use words like that, and my insides turn to mush, and I think about canoodling!"

"Keep that thought in mind. We'll have supper and sneak up the stairs to canoodle for a while."

She giggled. "The children make everything a little more difficult, but I wouldn't trade them for the world."

Bernard stopped the buggy in front of the foundling home. As he jumped down to help Elizabeth to the ground, she drew his head down for a quick kiss. "You're a better man than I deserve, Bernard Tandy."

Without waiting for a response, Elizabeth hurried up to the front door of the home, opening the door and calling out.

Within moments, both Mrs. Jackson and Amy had joined her in the parlor.

"Listen to this," Elizabeth said, unable to keep the elation from her voice as she read parts of the letter aloud. "Susan is thrilled! And she assures us they'll make arrangements for the girls, even though the specifics are yet to be worked out."

Mrs. Jackson, who had been watching Elizabeth with a mixture of anticipation and fondness, sighed in relief. "Bless her. That's one worry off our minds then."

"It is," Elizabeth replied, folding the letter with care. "We're set for Texas. Our little adventure is about to begin."

Amy shook her head. "I don't know if I should be happy or shaking in my boots."

Elizabeth smiled. "We'll find the perfect man for you."

Chapter Three

Amy Brown stood at the threshold of the foundling home, her hands clasped tightly in front of her. Her gaze swept over the sea of young, upturned faces that had become like family to her. A bright-eyed little girl tugged at the hem of Amy's skirt, her small fingers clinging with reluctance.

"Will you come back for us, Amy?" the child asked.

"If I can, Lily," Amy assured her, bending down to envelop the girl in a warm embrace. "I'll write letters, and one day, when I have a home as big as my dreams, there'll be a room waiting for each of you." She kissed the top of Lily's head, then stood to face the rest of the children, her eyes glistening but her smile unwavering.

"Remember what I always say," she said. "'No matter where we go, we carry a piece of each other's hearts.' So, be good to Mrs. Jackson, okay?"

"Okay, Amy!" they chimed in unison.

With a final wave, Amy turned away, hefting her modest carpetbag over her shoulder. The morning sun cast a golden hue across the Massachusetts landscape, heralding the dawn of her new adventure.

As she approached the wagon where eight other women awaited, a sense of camaraderie washed over her. These were her sisters in all but blood, each having grown under the same roof of the foundling home. Their faces mirrored Amy's own emotions: excitement and uncertainty. It was so strange to feel both at the same time.

"Ready to make our mark, ladies?" Amy called out.

"Ready as we'll ever be!" Brenda replied, her hands gripping the wooden edge of the wagon.

"Imagine, Fort Worth!" Faith said, her words carrying the thrill of possibility.

"Think of all the baking I can do there," Amy mused aloud, already picturing the kitchen she would one day call her own. "Cakes, pies, bread...enough to feed a dozen kids, at least."

Laughter bubbled among them, an easy sound that mingled with the creak of the wagon wheels as they rolled forward.

"No kids for me," Cassandra said. "I've had enough of kids in the foundling home and then teaching." She shuddered. "If I never have to touch another child, it will be too soon."

"Speak for yourself," Amy shot back playfully. "I'm after a family, not just a husband."

"Those sound like the same thing to me," Faith said.

As the foundling home shrank behind them, Amy's thoughts drifted to the future—a future ripe with the promise of love and a home brimming with laughter.

LESS THAN A WEEK LATER, the girls arrived in Fort Worth. The train ride, which had been so exciting at first, had turned into sheer monotony. Amy had spent her time making herself two aprons that covered the entire front of her dress. "I can't wait to make my husband breakfast," she said softly to Brenda.

"I'm more enthusiastic about the marital bed than I am about cooking," Brenda said. "I'm really excited to see how it feels when he..." She shook her head. "Sorry, sometimes my words get away from me."

Amy laughed softly. She and Brenda had discussed the same topic more times than she could count. Just not within earshot of Mrs. Jackson, who they all thought of as a mother. "Only two more stops and we're there. We have to go through Dallas, and then it's Fort Worth! Elizabeth said her sister Susan will be waiting at the train station with their biggest wagon, and their other sister Alice will be there with a wagon as well."

"Have you heard when the party will be?" Brenda asked.

Amy shook her head. "Even if I had, I couldn't tell you," she said. "You can't keep a secret to save your life."

"So it's a secret?" Brenda asked.

"Not that I know of."

Brenda sighed. "Sometimes I just want to slap you, and then I remember how much I love you, and I don't."

"I appreciate that you control yourself," Amy said, and the two dissolved into giggles. Brenda was closest in age to Amy, and they felt like they were real sisters, both of them twenty-two and the first of the children who had arrived at the home after Mrs. Jackson took over. Mrs. Jackson had named the girls according to the alphabet. The nine of them were: Amy, Brenda, Cassandra, Deborah, Erna, Faith, Gail, Hannah, and Imogene.

Some of the children came to the home with their names. Some had to be named. The ones who didn't already have a name were given the last name Brown.

At the train station in Fort Worth, there were two women waiting, but they looked more like mother and daughter than sisters. What was the age difference in Elizabeth's family?

Brenda and Amy both ended up in Alice's wagon, so Brenda asked. "Are you sure Susan is your sister and not your mother?"

Amy looked at her friend, hissing, "That's rude!"

Alice simply laughed. "Susan is the oldest and there are sixteen of us. I'm much younger, and she's actually my step-mother-in-law as well as my sister."

"What's a step-mother-in-law?" Amy asked. She'd never heard anyone use that phrase.

Alice grinned. "Susan moved west because she was tired of being the oldest of twelve children who were all unruly and acted crazy. In town, they called us the Demon Horde."

Brenda gasped. "You guys are legendary!"

"We really are. Do you believe only the youngest is unmarried now?" Alice shook her head. "I digress. Susan agreed to come west as a mail-order bride to marry Jesse Dailey. When she arrived, Jesse had been killed, and his brother David greeted her at the train station. David asked her to marry him. He had four boys already, and she insisted on meeting all of them before she'd agree, because let's face it, we were difficult to be around."

"I'll say!" Brenda said, awe in her voice.

"Anyway, David bribed his older boys to behave all through the meal. She agreed to marry him. It wasn't until the wedding was over that the boys were fighting in the streets and rolling in mud."

Amy sighed. "That was so unfair to her!"

"It was." Alice shook her head. "They were already married, so she stayed with him. I married David's oldest son, Albert, who is my step-nephew, but I'd never even met him, so it wasn't a problem."

"Is Susan happy now?" Amy asked.

"Oh, she has been for ages. She and David are a true love match. And so are Albert and I. But that makes her my sister and my mother-in-law. Strange, isn't it?"

"Very," Brenda agreed as Alice pulled up in front of a beautiful home. "Is this yours?"

Alice laughed. "No, I live in a little cabin on the ranch's land. This is Susan and David's house."

"It's beautiful," Amy said, admiring it.

"It is. I love it."

Alice jumped down from the wagon, and the girls in it followed suit.

Brenda put her hand on Alice's arm. "The party? Do you know when it is?"

Alice grinned. "Tomorrow night at seven. At the church."

"So if any of us marry there, it'll be a church wedding?" Hannah asked, sounding disappointed.

"I guess so," Alice replied.

ELIZABETH TANDY HAD outdone herself, Amy thought, as she took in the tastefully decorated space, festooned with ribbons and fresh flowers. The wooden floor gleamed underfoot, polished to a shine, ready for tentative steps and hopeful hearts.

They'd had supper with Susan and her family at five, and they were there for the night, as far as Amy could tell. She was excited though. Her first real dance.

Oh, she'd learned to dance in the orphanage. Mrs. Jackson had tried to make sure they had all the skills children with two parents had, and she'd danced with her "brothers" many times. But this would be real. She could dance with a man she just might marry.

"Quite something, isn't it?" Amy whispered to Brenda, her eyes wide with a blend of awe and nerves.

"Never seen anything like it," came the hushed reply, just as awestruck.

Amy's gaze flitted across the room, her fingers playing with the fabric of her dress—a subtle shade of blue that brought out the warmth in her cheeks. Men of Fort Worth mingled about, their postures ranging from confident struts to shy shuffles.

"Remember, breathe," Erna reminded her gently.

Amy let out a breath she hadn't realized she'd been holding and managed a grateful smile.

Then, amid the sea of faces, a particular figure caught her attention. He stood somewhat apart from the others. His hair was neatly combed, and he wore a black suit with a white shirt. He sipped his drink slowly, observing the crowd through guarded eyes that seemed to hold a reservoir of unspoken sorrow.

"Who's that?" Amy asked, nodding subtly toward the somber cowboy.

"Timothy Stockwell. Lost his wife last year," Elizabeth's voice carried softly from behind her. "Loves his children, but the poor man's lost with how to raise them."

Amy watched as Timothy offered a polite nod while maintaining a distance that discouraged any prolonged interaction. It was clear he was not at ease at the social event.

"Is he a rancher?" Amy asked. At Elizabeth's nod, she smiled. "Looks like he could use some cheering up," Amy murmured, more to herself than anyone else.

"Or a good pie," joked Imogene eliciting a round of chuckles from the group.

"Maybe both," Amy replied, the corner of her mouth quirking up.

"Go on then," urged another of the women with a gentle nudge. "See if your baking talk warms him up."

With a deep inhale of resolve, Amy smoothed down her dress and prepared to step into the unknown, her heart skipping to the rhythm of new beginnings.

Amy took a tentative step toward Timothy, the distant look in his eyes suggesting he was a world away from the bustle of Elizabeth Tandy's social. "Mr. Stockwell?" Her voice wavered slightly but found strength as he turned to her.

"Miss...?" He left the question hanging.

"Amy Brown," she replied, feeling the weight of the moment settle upon her shoulders. "From the foundling home in Massachusetts."

"Ah, one of Susan's sisters' ladies," Timothy nodded, a polite acknowledgment rather than genuine interest, yet something flickered behind his eyes—a spark of curiosity, perhaps.

"Yes," Amy said, searching for common ground. "I hear you have a ranch. Must be lovely, working with the land and animals."

"Nothing like it," he admitted, a sliver of warmth breaking through the clouds of his demeanor. "But it's a demanding life, not for the faint of heart."

"I've never been afraid of hard work," Amy said. "And I...I adore children."

"Is that so?" The corners of Timothy's mouth twitched upward, the first hint of a smile. "Kids are a handful, especially when they're your own." He paused, looking her over as if seeing her for the first time. "You think you're up for such a challenge?"

"More than you know," Amy answered, her spirit rising to the surface. "I've always dreamed of a big family."

The air between them became charged, laced with possibilities. They were strangers, yet in that brief exchange, there was an unspoken understanding.

"Big families mean big meals," Timothy said after a moment, his tone lightened by the prospect. "They tell me you can cook."

"Only if you consider baking pies an essential skill," she teased back, her nervousness giving way to a budding connection.

"Essential? In Texas, Miss Brown, pie is practically currency."

As laughter escaped her lips, Amy felt the fluttering in her chest evolve into a warm glow. Here was a man who could appreciate her love for the simple things—family, food, and the comfort of home.

But as the laughter faded, doubts crept in, wrapping cold fingers around her heart. Marrying a man she had just met was madness, wasn't it? Yet as she looked into Timothy's eyes, filled with a mixture of hope and sorrow, she couldn't help but wonder if this was the leap of faith she was meant to take.

"Family's everything to me," she confessed, her voice barely above a whisper. "But I'd be lying if I said I wasn't scared."

"Scared?" Timothy repeated, his brow furrowing in empathy. "Of what?"

"Of making a mistake. Of choosing a life that might not be..." She trailed off, unsure how to voice the fear of the unknown.

"Right," he finished for her, nodding slowly. "It's a gamble for both of us."

"Yet here we are," Amy said, meeting his gaze squarely, "considering rolling the dice."

"Seems so," Timothy agreed, the ghost of a smile returning. "Life's full of gambles."

Amy's mind raced with the enormity of the decision before her. Could she really marry this man and build a life with him out of nothing but hope and a few shared words? The very thought sent a thrill of excitement mixed with trepidation coursing through her.

"Maybe," she ventured, her voice steady despite the turmoil within, "it's about finding someone just as willing to take that risk with you."

"Maybe," Tim repeated, and in that simple word, Amy heard the echo of her own longing—a desire for companionship, for love, and the chance to create the family she had always yearned for.

TIMOTHY'S HAND INSTINCTIVELY found the brim of his hat, fingers fumbling with the rough fabric—a habit when thoughts clouded his mind. He watched Amy mingle with others, her laughter a melody that seemed both hopeful and haunting.

"Mind if I steal you away for a moment?" His voice was steady as he approached her, but inside, Tim wrestled with doubt. The fresh memory of love lost gnawed at his resolve.

"Of course," Amy replied.

They stepped out onto the porch, the night air crisp, the sky a blanket of stars. Alone now, Timothy hesitated, the weight of his decision pressing down like the Texas heat.

"Beautiful night," Amy ventured, breaking the silence between them.

"Reminds me of..." Tim began, then trailed off.

"Of what?" she prompted gently, sensing the shift in his demeanor.

"Of a time before." The words came out as a whisper. "Before my world turned upside down."

Amy's eyes softened, reflecting the moonlight. "Loss changes us," she murmured. "It leaves spaces that never quite fill the same way again."

"Exactly." Timothy felt the knot in his chest loosen slightly. "I worry about making promises when I'm still picking up pieces."

"Maybe," Amy said, "we're not meant to pick them up alone."

Her words hung between them, an invitation and a solace. In that shared quiet, Timothy felt the barriers he'd built crumble piece by piece.

"Can I tell you a secret?" Amy leaned closer.

"Anything," he assured her, drawn to the honesty in her eyes.

"I'm terrified." A half-smile played on her lips. "Terrified of choosing wrong, of taking a step that can't be undone."

"Seems we're two sides of the same coin, then." Timothy's chuckle was soft, mingling with hers.

"Perhaps we are," she agreed. "But sometimes...I think maybe it's less about the steps we take and more about who's walking beside us."

"Maybe you're right. Perhaps together, we could find a rhythm that works—one step at a time."

"Wouldn't that be something?"

"It would." Timothy extended his hand, palm open and waiting. "Shall we start with this dance?"

Amy placed her hand in his.

AMY'S LAUGHTER FADED into the soft evening air as Elizabeth Tandy approached with a gentle smile. The blonde-haired matchmaker placed a reassuring hand upon Amy's shoulder.

"Dear, I see more than just shared glances and quiet confessions between you two," Elizabeth said, her green eyes twinkling. "There is potential for something truly beautiful."

Tim fidgeted with the brim of his hat, an artifact of nervousness that he couldn't quite shake. "I think there's a heap of uncertainty in all this, Mrs. Tandy," he admitted.

"Life's full of uncertainties, Mr. Stockwell. It's the courage to face them that makes love worthwhile." Elizabeth's voice carried the wisdom of someone who had fostered countless unions. "Sometimes, taking a chance on love is the very thing that gives us strength."

Amy glanced at Tim, finding strength in Elizabeth's words. "She's right, Tim," she said softly. "We might just be better together than we are apart."

He met her gaze, the corners of his mouth lifting ever so slightly. "Could be. But it's a mighty big decision, marrying someone you've only just met."

"True," she conceded. "But I'd rather take a leap of faith with someone who understands the value of family, who yearns for it, just like I do."

"Family..." Timothy repeated. "I'd like that too."

"Then why not build one together?" There was a hopeful audacity in Amy's proposition.

"Build it together, huh?" His eyes searched hers.

"Elizabeth," Amy started, "we've decided. We're going to marry."

"Marvelous!" Elizabeth clasped her hands together. "You've both got caring hearts and strong spirits. You'll be happy together."

"Thank you, ma'am. For believing in us," Timothy said.

"Belief is easy when you see what I see," Elizabeth replied. "Now go on, make a life that's as sweet as one of Amy's pies."

With that, Tim extended his arm to Amy. "Well, partner, shall we start planning for our dozen or so little ones?"

"Let's not get ahead of ourselves," Amy laughed, linking her arm with his. "One step at a time."

"Fair enough," Timothy chuckled. "One step at a time."

Amy clasped her hands together, a gesture that mirrored the flutter of excitement in her chest. As she stood under the wide-open Texas sky beside Timothy, she could almost touch the dreams that danced before her eyes—a cozy home filled with the warmth of a family she'd call her own.

"Imagine it, Tim," she said. "A little house, maybe one with a porch where we can watch the sunset."

"Sounds perfect," Timothy replied, his smile reaching his eyes. "My children will be awful happy to have a homecooked meal that I didn't cook. "

Her heart skipped at the thought. "I look forward to getting to know them." Amy's laughter mingled with the soft evening breeze, light and carefree.

"Children with your kindness," Timothy added softly, his gaze holding hers. "I hope you know how to teach that kindness."

"Tim..." She reached out, her hand finding his, their fingers intertwining naturally. "I can hardly believe this is happening. That we're doing this—together."

"Me neither, Amy." He squeezed her hand gently. "But I'm grateful. Grateful for you, for this chance at a new start."

"Me too." She leaned closer, her head resting against his shoulder. "We've got a whole life ahead of us, Tim. It's like we're standing on the edge of a brand-new day."

"Then let's step into it," he whispered.

"Absolutely," she agreed, her heart brimming with hope for every tomorrow they would share.

"MRS. JACKSON?" AMY called out when she spotted the older woman.

The matron turned from where she had been talking to some of the other girls. "Yes, my dear?" Mrs. Jackson asked.

"I've made my decision," Amy said.

Mrs. Jackson's face softened into a knowing smile. "You're going to marry him, aren't you?"

Amy nodded, a blush coloring her cheeks. "Yes, I am. Tim is…he's good, and kind. And I think we could make each other happy."

"Then that's all that matters." Mrs. Jackson enveloped Amy in a warm embrace. "Tim will be a lucky man to have you by his side."

"Thank you," Amy whispered, holding back the tears that threatened to spill over. "For everything."

"Promise me one thing," Mrs. Jackson said as they parted. "Make sure he takes care of my baby girl."

"I will, Mrs. Jackson. I promise."

Timothy stood beside Amy, his hat held nervously in his hands. He looked from Amy to Mrs. Jackson, a question in his eyes.

"Tim," Mrs. Jackson addressed him. "Take care of her. She's precious to us all."

Tim's gaze met Amy's, and she saw the solemn vow there before he spoke. "I will, ma'am. I'll do my very best."

"Good." A satisfied nod from Mrs. Jackson, and then she shooed them both toward the front of the church. "Now off you go. Pastor Amos is waiting to make an honest couple out of you."

Pastor Amos Kauffman greeted them with a gentle smile, his eyes reflecting the sanctity of the moment. Amy had met the pastor earlier that evening, but she didn't feel the same things she felt when she looked at Tim.

"Are you ready to take this step together?" he asked.

"Yes, sir, we are," they answered in unison, their voices intermingling like threads in a finely woven quilt.

"Then let's begin." Amos opened his well-worn Bible and began the ceremony that would bind Amy and Timothy in marriage.

"Timothy, do you take Amy to be your lawfully wedded wife, to cherish in love and companionship?"

"I do," Tim replied, his voice resolute.

"And Amy, do you take Timothy to be your lawfully wedded husband, to cherish in love and companionship?"

"I do," she repeated, her heart soaring.

"By the power vested in me," Amos continued, "I now pronounce you husband and wife."

As Amos closed the Bible, the simplicity of the ceremony felt perfect. The vows spoken were not just words; they were the seeds of a future they would cultivate together.

"May I kiss the bride?" Tim asked, a hopeful twinkle in his eye.

"Of course," Amy laughed, light and free.

The kiss made Amy feel things she'd heard Brenda whispering about, though how Brenda knew things like that, she didn't know. For now, she was happy. She had met the man she'd have a family with.

Chapter Four

It was dark as Amy and Tim made their way to the ranch. The house was still with all the children in bed. Amy's heart fluttered, her hand finding Tim's in the dark. They shared a look, one brimming with promises and secret smiles.

"Seems the little ones are all dreaming," Tim whispered, his voice low and warm against her ear.

Amy nodded, her cheeks flushed with anticipation. In the quiet privacy of his bedroom, they came together with urgency. Tim's hands were gentle, his touch reverent, as if he understood the significance of the moment. For Amy, it was a whirlwind of sensation, a connection that rooted deep within her soul. She clung to Tim as if he were her anchor in the storm of emotions that swept through her.

And when it was over, when the tremors of new intimacy had subsided, there lay a serene excitement for what the next day would bring. Amy couldn't wait to meet his children.

AMY WOKE BEFORE ANYONE else and after dressing in the dark, she went to the kitchen to start breakfast. She hoped to meet his children that morning, and she wanted the first meal she cooked for the family to be perfect. Beatrice sat at the table, her expression sour as Amy hummed a tune and moved around with ease.

"You must be Beatrice," Amy said, casting a warm smile toward the girl. "How about we bake some cookies later? It's something I've always loved doing."

"Cookies?" Beatrice mumbled, eyeing the flour-dusted counter with skepticism.

"Yep! We could make a whole batch, just for us and your sisters." Amy's eyes sparkled with thought. "I think it would be a fun way for us to get to know each other."

"Fun..." Beatrice repeated, her voice trailing off. Finally, she shrugged. "I guess I like cookies."

Amy laughed. "Of course you like cookies!"

Tim's son walked into the room then, and Amy searched her mind for his name. *George. He'd said the boy was George.* "Good morning, George. I hope you're hungry!" Amy flipped some pancakes onto a plate, added bacon, and told him to sit, putting the plate on the table in front of him. Amy paused. "I didn't think to ask. Do you usually have breakfast in the kitchen or the dining room?"

George quickly swallowed a bite of bacon so he could respond. "Kitchen."

"Oh, good. I guessed right!"

Two small heads popped around the corner, staring at her. "I'm your new stepmother, Amy."

Priscilla stared at Amy for a moment. "Are you evil like Cinderella's stepmother?"

Amy laughed. "I am not. I'm happy to have the four of you in my life. I always wanted at least a dozen children."

Beatrice frowned, pushing the plate away. "You're not our mother."

Amy nodded. "No, I'm not. But I will try my best to treat you like you are my children."

"Try all you want, but Ma will always be our mother!" Beatrice said, running from the room.

Amy stared after her for a moment. She thought about going after her, but that didn't seem like it would be helpful. Instead, she put pancakes and bacon on plates for Ruby and Priscilla.

"Have you seen your pa this morning?" Amy asked.

George shook his head. "He gets the milking done before he eats breakfast." He stuck another piece of bacon into his mouth. "Probably getting the eggs too."

"Perfect, then I can bake a cake and make cookies today. I thought we'd have to choose one or the other."

"Cake?" Ruby asked. "You're going to bake a cake?"

"I sure am. And I'll make some frosting for it. We'll call it a celebration." Amy could see there was a lot of work to be done around the house that didn't involve baking, but that was fine with her. She felt useful and needed, and it was good to feel that way. "If you have dirty clothes or something that needs to be mended, please bring it into the kitchen for me. I'll need to tackle laundry when I finish with the breakfast dishes."

Priscilla smiled. "Can I help with the dishes? Ma always told me I wasn't quite old enough."

Amy smiled, nodding. "I'd love to have you as my dish apprentice."

Ruby frowned. "I could help too."

"Yes, of course. We'll all do it together. Many hands make for light work!"

The kitchen door opened and closed, and Amy looked up at her new husband. It felt strange seeing him in daylight after what they'd done in the dark the night before, but she refused to look away. "Hungry?" she asked.

He sniffed the air and washed his hands quickly. "I am as hungry as any man who hasn't had a decent meal in a year."

Amy shook her head. "From now on, we'll shoot for decent meals three times per day." As he sat, she put his breakfast in front of him and served her own. "Does anyone else need anything before I start my own meal?"

When no one responded, Amy took her plate to the table and ate. Nothing tasted better than bacon and coffee in the mornings.

"What do you have planned for the day?" Tim asked.

"I'm going to get laundry on the line, bake cookies with Beatrice, bake a cake for dessert tonight, and I'll figure out a meal I can make. Do some mending and cleaning as I have time."

"That sounds like a lot right there. George and I are usually home for lunch around noon, and supper around five. I prefer to milk at five in the morning and five in the evening."

"Sounds good to me," she said. "I'll make sure I have meals ready at those times."

Within minutes, both Tim and George had finished eating and were out the door. Amy took the laundry that had been brought down, quickly realizing that Beatrice hadn't brought hers down, but she wasn't sure if the girl had been in the kitchen when she'd asked for laundry.

Amy hurried up the stairs to the door that was closed. It had to be Beatrice's room. She knocked and waited. Beatrice came to the door, the same sullen look on her face that had been there at breakfast, but it was obvious she'd been crying. "What?"

"I need your laundry. Anything dirty or that needs mending."

Beatrice turned around, walked into her room, and came back with a huge mound of clothing. "There. Happy now?"

"I'm always happy," Amy said with a smile, taking the laundry.

Doing the laundry took a lot longer than Amy had anticipated. She'd expected it to take a fraction of time it took at the foundling home, but this family had a lot more clothes per person than the orphans did, and it seemed everything they owned was dirty.

As soon as it was all on the line, she fixed a simple lunch. She served it at the table in the dining room, hoping that was where they ate their lunches. School was out for the summer, and she was grateful for time with the children.

When the lunch dishes were done, and her two small helpers were off to play, Amy told them to ask Beatrice to come to the kitchen.

Beatrice scrunched her nose as Amy laid out the ingredients on the kitchen table. "I don't see what's so great about cookies," she said, crossing her arms over her chest. "And I doubt you can bake them as well as Mama did."

Amy brushed a strand of hair from her forehead. "Well, every batch is unique, just like the person who bakes them," she replied with an unwavering smile. "Why don't we give it a try together? You might find you have a knack for it."

"Me? Help?" Beatrice scoffed, eyeing the sugar and flour sacks. "I'd probably just mess it up."

"Everyone starts somewhere," Amy said, picking up a measuring cup and offering it to Beatrice. "How about you measure the flour while I get the eggs? We'll take it one step at a time."

Reluctantly, Beatrice uncrossed her arms and took the cup, her fingers brushing against Amy's. "Fine, but only because you look like you need all the help you can get," she muttered.

"Thank you, Beatrice. I'm sure you'll be a tremendous help." Amy's voice was earnest, her eyes kind. She guided Beatrice's hand to the flour sack. "We need two cups, leveled off just right."

Beatrice dipped the cup into the flour. She squinted, trying to level the top as Amy had instructed.

"See? You're a natural," Amy encouraged, her tone light and cheery. "Now, could you pass me the butter? We'll need to cream it with the sugar next."

With a hesitant nod, Beatrice slid the block of butter across the table. The kitchen was warm, the air filled with the scent of potential sweets. She watched Amy work the mixture and found herself leaning in, curiosity edging out her reluctance.

"All right, your turn again," Amy said, handing Beatrice a wooden spoon. "Do you want to stir for a bit?"

"Sure," Beatrice replied, a half-smile tugging at her lips. "But if this turns out bad, it's not my fault."

"I'll take any blame needed," Amy said. "But I have a feeling these cookies are going to be something special, just like us."

Beatrice's arm moved in steady circles, stirring the butter and sugar mixture while Amy greased the cookie sheets. The clinking of the spoon against the bowl set a rhythm in the cozy kitchen.

"Does it always take this long to cream together?" Beatrice asked, glancing over her shoulder at Amy with an impatience that was beginning to give way to intrigue.

"Patience is key in baking," Amy replied, wiping her hands on her apron. "Just like when I was at the foundling home. We'd all gather 'round, each taking turns, telling stories while we waited for our turn to mix."

"Sounds...fun," Beatrice said, though the word seemed foreign on her lips.

"It was," Amy smiled, watching the younger girl work. "We didn't have much, but those moments made us feel like we had everything."

"Everything?" Beatrice repeated, her voice softening.

"Yep, every laugh, every burnt cookie—it was ours. Made the place feel like home."

The wooden spoon paused mid-stir as Beatrice mulled over Amy's words. Then, with a slight shrug, she resumed her task. "What else did you bake?"

"Everything from bread to biscuits. But cookies? They were my favorite." Amy's eyes twinkled with the memories. "They were easy enough for us to try out different things—raisins, nuts, sometimes even bits of candy if we were lucky."

"Did they ever turn out strange?" Beatrice's lips curled into a genuine smile.

"Strange and wonderful," Amy laughed. "Like the time we mixed in too much salt instead of sugar. We couldn't stop laughing, even though they were awful."

"Guess that means these could be worse." Beatrice glanced down at the dough with a new sense of possibility.

"Exactly," Amy agreed, rolling up her sleeves. "Now, how about we add some cinnamon? Gives them a nice warmth."

"Sure," Beatrice nodded, reaching for the spice herself. "How much?"

"Let's start with a teaspoon and see how we feel."

Amy handed Beatrice a wooden spoon, the handle worn smooth from years of use. "Here, why don't you do the honors? You need to spoon the cookies onto the pan."

"Like this?" Beatrice asked, her fingers curling around the spoon as she put a spoonful of dough onto the pan.

"Perfect," Amy praised, watching the girl's careful movements. She leaned back against the counter, observing Beatrice come alive in the warmth of the kitchen. "You've got a good touch. Your mama must have spent a lot of time with you in the kitchen."

Beatrice paused, her eyes lingering on the golden batter. "She did...before." Her voice trailed off, lost in the bittersweet tang of memories.

"Before?"

"Before she got sick." Beatrice dropped her gaze, focusing intently on the mixing bowl.

Amy reached out, laying a gentle hand on Beatrice's shoulder. "I can't imagine how hard that must have been for you."

Beatrice shrugged. "It was fine. I mean, I had to learn to help with my sisters and all."

"Fine isn't the same as easy, though, is it?" Amy's question hung softly between them.

"Nothing's been easy." Beatrice said.

"Change never is," Amy said, her voice a soothing balm. "But sometimes, it brings something good too. Like new friends, or...new family."

"Is that what we are now? Family?" There was hope mixed with the skepticism in Beatrice's tone.

"If you want us to be," Amy replied earnestly. "I know I'm not your mama, Beatrice, and I don't aim to replace her. But I'd like to think she'd be happy knowing her girls were loved and cared for."

"Maybe." A single tear rolled down Beatrice's cheek before she hastily wiped it away.

"Hey," Amy said gently, tilting Beatrice's chin up to meet her eyes. "It's okay to miss her. And it's okay to be scared. But I promise, you're not alone anymore."

"Promise?" The word was a whisper.

"Cross my heart."

"Okay." Beatrice nodded, a fragile smile breaking through. "Okay."

Later, while the aroma of freshly baked cookies filled the air. Amy poured hot water into two teacups, the gentle clink of ceramic against ceramic punctuating the comfortable silence that had settled between her and Beatrice.

"Smells like heaven," Amy remarked, smiling as she set a cup before Beatrice. The girl looked up.

"Thank you," Beatrice murmured, cradling the cup in her hands.

"Nothing beats a good batch of cookies and a cup of tea," Amy said, taking a seat across from Beatrice. She sipped her tea, thinking with as hot it was in Texas in June, she should have chosen to make ice tea.

"Guess it's all right," Beatrice conceded. "I think I'd still rather have milk, though."

The door creaked open, and Ruby slipped into the room, followed by a bounding Priscilla. Their eyes were wide, drawn to the promise of treats and the comforting ritual of teatime.

"Can we have some?" Ruby asked, her voice soft but hopeful.

"Of course." Amy's heart swelled at the sight of the young girls. She fetched two more cups and poured half tea, half milk, knowing full well the strength of the brew could be too much for their young taste buds.

"Here you go." She slid the cups toward them, earning gleeful grins in return.

"Thank you, Amy!" Priscilla chirped, gripping her cup with both hands.

Beatrice watched her sisters, her gaze lingering on Amy's face as she interacted with them. A shadow crossed her features.

"Hey," Amy caught Beatrice's eye. "There's plenty of love to go around."

"Sure," Beatrice said, though her voice was less than convinced.

"Really, Beatrice," Amy continued, sensing the need to affirm her commitment. "You're not losing anything. We're just making our family bigger, that's all."

"Family," Beatrice repeated softly.

"Exactly," Amy replied.

The young girl's eyes, previously sparkling with reluctant mirth, now held a glint of something else—resentment, perhaps, or fear.

"Enjoy your tea...with them," Beatrice said, her voice tight as she jerked her chin toward Ruby and Priscilla.

Beatrice bolted, her chair screeching against the wooden floorboards in protest. "You're probably just going to die anyway!" She dashed through the doorway, her footsteps echoing down the hallway.

Amy started to rise, her instinct to comfort and chase after the upset child tugging at her. But she paused, her hand hovering mid-air. Maybe, just maybe, Beatrice needed space more than soothing words right now.

"Will she be okay?" Ruby asked, peering up at Amy, her big eyes round with concern.

"Sure, she will," Amy replied. "Sometimes we all need a moment to ourselves, don't we?"

"Like when I hide in the barn?" Priscilla asked.

"Exactly like that," Amy agreed, wishing she had something magic to heal this broken family.

Amy turned her attention back to the littler girls. "Shall we pack up some cookies for Papa and George?" she asked, brushing aside her concerns about Beatrice.

"Can we put 'em in the pail?" Ruby suggested.

"Sure thing," Amy agreed. She stood up, collecting the golden-brown treats from the cooling rack. Together, they lined the bottom of the pail with a clean cloth before stacking the cookies neatly inside.

They found Tim and George near the barn, deep in conversation about the next day's chores.

"Pa! George!" Ruby called out, swinging the pail as they approached.

"Is that for us?" Tim asked, his eyes lighting up at the sight of his daughters and Amy approaching with the pail.

"Did you make these, Amy?" George asked, eagerly reaching for a cookie as soon as the lid was lifted.

"It was a team effort," Amy responded, glancing down at Ruby and Priscilla, who beamed with pride.

"Best cookies I've ever had!" Tim praised.

"Let's not let them get cold," George said, grinning as he grabbed another.

"Try one, Amy," Tim urged, extending the pail toward her.

"I had my fill with the girls. All of those are for the two of you," Amy said softly.

"Girls, let's leave the pail with them," Amy said softly. "We can pick it up later."

"Okay, Amy," Priscilla replied, slipping her hand into Amy's as they started back toward the house.

"More cookies tomorrow?" Ruby asked, looking up at Amy with hopeful eyes.

"Absolutely," Amy promised, squeezing Ruby's hand gently. Things weren't as rosy as Amy had imagined, but they'd get there. She was certain of it!

Chapter Five

Amy Stockwell sat on the modest porch of the house, her hands twisting a handkerchief in her lap. She was waiting for Brenda and Cassandra, her heart sisters from the orphanage, now her neighbors and closest allies.

"Lord knows I need their counsel," she murmured, thinking of Beatrice's cold stares and sharp words. Amy's heart was full of love, but she wasn't certain Beatrice was ready to accept that love from her.

"Troubles?" Brenda's voice called out as she approached the porch, Cassandra followed Brenda as they both climbed the steps to the porch and sat down in the wooden chairs there, and Amy marveled for the millionth time about just how short Cassandra was.

"Every day's a battle with Beatrice, Tim's oldest daughter," Amy confided, once they were all seated on the creaky wooden planks, the scent of fresh-cut grass filling the air. "She's twelve and looks at me like I'm trying to erase her mama's memory."

"It sounds like she's still grieving her mama," Brenda said. "But even the wildest storm can be calmed."

Cassandra leaned forward, placing a comforting hand on Amy's knee. "Mrs. Jackson," she began, "she always had a way with the older girls who lost their mothers. She'd listen more than she'd talk, let them cry until the tears wouldn't come anymore."

"Did it work?" Amy asked, hope flickering in her chest.

"I never saw it fail," Cassandra replied with a smile. "Sometimes, a heart just needs to know it's heard."

"Wouldn't hurt to try," Amy said softly.

Brenda cocked her head to one side, her eyes sparkling with an idea. "Here's what you do, Amy," she began, a playful lilt in her voice, "why not take Beatrice out for a walk? The blackberries are ripe for picking. A basket each, and you'll have your hands too full of berries to fret."

Amy's brow arched in surprise, her gaze fixed on the sprawling fields beyond their homestead. She nodded thoughtfully, picturing the brambles heavy with fruit. "I do love a good blackberry pie," she mused.

"Exactly," Brenda declared with a grin, clapping her hands together. "Nothing sweetens a sour mood like a bit of sunshine and berry juice staining your fingers."

Cassandra, who had been quietly listening, softly cleared her throat. "Remember, it's not just about the berries," she said gently. "Beatrice needs patience and someone to simply be there. I've felt that same emptiness, never having known my mother."

Amy nodded slowly. "I won't rush her," she promised, her voice steady. " I'll walk beside her."

"Then it's settled," Brenda said, clapping her hands in finality. "Tomorrow, you two will pick all the blackberries in Texas."

"Thank you," Amy whispered. She clasped a steaming cup of tea, the scent of chamomile rising with the morning mist. "Can I truly make a difference?"

Brenda leaned against the porch railing, her gaze softening as she regarded Amy. "You know, you don't have to be her mother to be someone important in her life," she said.

"I fear she sees me trying to step into shoes far too cherished to ever be filled by another," Amy confessed.

"Then let her know that," Brenda suggested. "Tell her you're here to add to her life, not to take anything—or anyone—away."

Amy agreed with her friend's suggestion. "I'll talk to her, heart to heart."

Cassandra emerged from the house, wiping her hands on her apron, the flour dusting her cheeks giving her a ghost of a blush. "You should try to schedule a day to spend alone with her." She took a seat beside Amy on the swing, the gentle creak of the chains joining their conversation.

"Alone?" Amy asked, unsure of how Beatrice would react.

"Sure," Cassandra continued, her tone matter-of-fact. "Just you and Beatrice. It might help her see you're not here to overshadow memories."

"New memories," Amy repeated softly. "We could start small. Perhaps a walk tomorrow? And the picnic and berry picking. Oh, and we can follow it up with pie baking!" Amy laughed. "Although I'm not sure that's starting small."

Cassandra patted Amy's knee, a gesture of solidarity. "Let her share her world with you, and in turn, share yours with her."

"Thank you, both of you," Amy said, relaxing as plans began to form. "I think…I think maybe that would work for us."

"Of course, it will," Brenda said, her blunt nature leaving no room for doubt. "Now go on, the day is young and full of promise."

AMY HOISTED THE WICKER basket onto her hip. It was a fine day for an outing, she mused. It was a bit too hot, but she was going to have to get used to hot if she was going to live in Texas. She approached Beatrice, who stood by the garden gate, her posture stiff as a fence post.

"Ready for an adventure?" Amy asked.

Beatrice's eyes met Amy's. "What sort of adventure?" Her tone was cautious.

"Something sweet," Amy hinted, tapping the basket. "There's a surprise inside for later."

With a reluctant nod, Beatrice swung the gate open, and they stepped onto the path that wound through the fields. They walked side by side, a comfortable silence settling between them like a quilt on a winter's night.

"Did I ever tell you about the time I tried to milk a cow backward?" Amy began.

"Backward?" Beatrice asked, an eyebrow arching in curiosity despite herself.

"Yes," Amy chuckled. "You see, I thought the stool was supposed to face the other way. Needless to say, Bessie the cow was not amused."

Beatrice's lips twitched, a hint of amusement threatening to bloom. Amy seized the moment, weaving tale after tale, each more preposterous than the last—of goats that danced jigs and chickens that laid square eggs.

As they meandered through the tall grass, Amy pointed out the blackberry bushes ahead. "Look at those berries! They're practically begging to be picked. What do you say?"

"Fine," Beatrice agreed.

They reached the thicket, and Amy handed Beatrice a small basket, their fingers brushing fleetingly. Beatrice watched as Amy deftly plucked the plump blackberries, her hands sure and gentle.

"Like this," Amy instructed, demonstrating. "Just be wary of the thorns. They can be sneaky."

Beatrice followed suit, her movements hesitant at first but growing more confident with each berry she freed from the vine. The sun dipped lower in the sky, casting golden threads over the field, turning an ordinary afternoon into something akin to magic.

"This afternoon," Amy ventured, "we could try our hand at baking a pie with these. What do you think?"

"Perhaps," Beatrice murmured.

After filling their baskets, they walked a little further. Amy paused. They had walked in silence for a stretch. She glanced at Beatrice, who seemed lost in thought, her basket of blackberries cradled against her chest.

"Beatrice," Amy said, "I haven't always had a family."

Beatrice looked up, curiosity flickering in her eyes.

"I grew up in a foundling home," Amy continued, picking a lone daisy from the grass and twirling it between her fingers. "No mother or father to speak of, but there were others like me. We liked to pretend we were a real family."

"Was it very bad?" Beatrice's question was hesitant, the words barely a whisper.

"Lonely at times," Amy admitted with a small smile. "But it taught me something valuable — that families come in all shapes and sizes. And love can be found in the most unexpected places."

Beatrice was silent for a moment before speaking again. "I'm scared, you know. Of everything changing. Of forgetting her." Her voice trembled slightly.

Amy reached out, placing a comforting hand on Beatrice's shoulder. "Your mother will always be a part of you, Beatrice. I could never take her place, nor would I want to. I'm just here to add to your life, not to erase what's been."

"Really?"

"Truly," Amy affirmed, squeezing Beatrice's shoulder reassuringly. "We'll find our way, you and I. For now, just think of me as a friend."

Stepping over the threshold of their home, Amy and Beatrice shared a private glance.

"Look at us," Amy said, "an afternoon well spent, wouldn't you say?"

Beatrice's lips curved into a tentative smile, the first genuine one Amy had seen. "I suppose it was better than I expected," she conceded.

"Better is good," Amy nodded, setting down her basket on the kitchen table. "Now, how about we get those little hands busy with some pie baking? I bet your sisters would love to join us."

"Really?" Beatrice's eyes widened. "You don't mind them helping?"

"Family means everyone contributes," Amy said warmly. "The more, the merrier. Besides, I've always believed that joy shared is joy doubled."

"All right." A flicker of excitement sparked within Beatrice as she set her own basket beside Amy's. With newfound eagerness, she turned toward the door. "I'll go fetch them!"

"Tell them there's a reward of pie at the end of their labor," Amy called after her, laughter dancing in her words.

"Will do!" Beatrice shouted back, eager to include her sisters in the newfound camaraderie.

Amy watched her go with a smile. She hoped their truce would hold for a good long while.

Chapter Six

Amy woke before dawn the following morning, and for a moment she lay in bed, watching Tim sleep for a moment. She wasn't sure she'd ever get used to waking up in bed with a man, but she sure did enjoy seeing him there.

Amy tossed the quilt aside and hopped to her feet. She quickly dressed in a simple cotton dress. Her fingers worked nimbly, buttoning up with practiced ease. The air outside already hinted at how very hot the day would be.

"Morning's too precious to waste," she whispered to herself.

Amy beelined for the chicken coop, where she had seen Tim collect their breakfast bounty. The hens clucked contentedly as she approached, as if they too appreciated the novelty of her company. She reached into the nesting boxes, her hands gentle but confident, gathering warm eggs into the folds of her apron.

"Good morning, ladies," she cooed to the hens. They responded with a chorus of approving clucks, seemingly charmed by her presence.

Back in the kitchen, Amy set about preparing breakfast with the same love and attention she'd given to every task since arriving at the ranch. The eggs were whipped into a frothy golden sea, and she folded in chunks of bacon. It was a simple meal, but Amy knew that after a year of trying to eat Tim's cooking, the entire family would appreciate it.

As the family gathered around the table, each face a canvas of sleep-smudged features slowly brightening with alertness, Amy served the scrambled eggs.

"Smells good, Amy," one of the younger girls murmured, her voice still thick with sleep.

"Thank you, darling," Amy replied, her heart swelling with pride. "Eat up now, we've got a full day ahead."

While the family ate, Amy's gaze roamed the room, noting the little touches that transformed the house into a home. Later, she'd get on her knees and give the kitchen floor a thorough scrubbing. A sense of belonging settled within her—a feeling she hadn't known she'd been missing until now. She wasn't living in a temporary home anymore. She was a wife and mother, and she had complete control of the house.

"Once I'm done in here," she thought, "I'll spend some time with Ruby and Priscilla." She couldn't help but look forward to the laughter and joy that the rest of the day promised.

AMY ROSE FROM HER KNEES, the bucket of murky water a testament to her morning's labor. She wiped a stray wisp of hair from her forehead with the back of her hand, feeling a sense of satisfaction as she surveyed the gleaming kitchen floor.

Stepping into the warmth of the day, Amy shielded her eyes and scanned the expanse of the property. There, by the barn, Ruby and Priscilla were immersed in a game of their own making, their laughter floating on the breeze like dandelion seeds.

"Ruby, Priscilla!" Amy called out, her voice carrying over the open space. Her heart quickened at the thought of sharing this day with them—the first of many, she hoped.

The two girls paused, glancing her way with expressions of curiosity. Ruby, ever the quiet one, seemed to weigh the invitation, her small fingers fiddling with the hem of her dress. Priscilla seemed excited at the idea of adventure, her young mind likely already racing ahead to the wonders they might discover.

"Come on, let's explore together! Have you seen the creek beyond the south meadow?" Amy's tone was light, imbued with an excitement she couldn't contain.

Ruby bit her lip, hesitating. "Is it far? Mama never let us go too far from the house."

"Not too far," Amy reassured, mindful to address Ruby's reserved nature with gentle encouragement. "And I've heard there's no better place on the ranch for skipping stones."

Priscilla was ready. The little daredevil was already bounding toward Amy, her small legs kicking up dust. "I want to see! Let's go!"

"Wait for me!" Ruby's voice held a newfound determination as she took off after her sister.

Amy led the way, her boots pressing into the soft earth of the dirt path. A chorus of morning birdsong filled the air, and she couldn't help but smile at the simple melody of the ranch coming to life.

"Look there," Amy pointed to a cluster of wildflowers. "Those are Indian Paintbrushes. Aren't they pretty?"

"Like paint on a canvas," Ruby murmured, her fingers grazing the fiery red blooms.

Priscilla, not to be outdone, chimed in with a grin, "And those little ones are Bluebonnets, right?"

"No," Amy said shaking her head. "Bluebonnets are only in bloom in March and April in this area."

They continued along the path, Amy sharing tidbits about the local flora and fauna, while the girls absorbed every word. She was glad she'd taken time to read a book about gardening in Texas she'd found on the bookshelf in the parlor. The simplicity of their walk, the shared curiosity—it felt like a promise of good things to come.

"Wow," Priscilla breathed out, eyes wide as saucers.

"Isn't it something?" Amy said, her gaze sweeping over the view.

Ruby nodded silently, caught up in the grandeur of it all.

Amy let out a wistful sigh, her heart swelling with a sense of belonging. "I wish I could paint," she said, almost to herself. "Then I'd capture this moment, keep it forever."

"Can't we just remember it?" Ruby asked, tilting her head.

"Of course, we can," Amy replied, ruffling Ruby's hair affectionately. "Memories are the best kind of keepsakes, aren't they?"

"Better than any painting," Priscilla agreed, beaming.

Together, they stood atop the hill, three souls bound by the beauty of the open land and the warmth of newfound companionship.

"Let's head over to the vegetable garden," Amy suggested, her eyes twinkling with a hint of adventure. "We can pick some fresh veggies for dinner."

"Really?" Ruby's voice quivered with excitement, her usual reserve melting away.

"Uh-huh!" Priscilla clapped her hands, bouncing on the balls of her feet.

"See these tomatoes?" Amy pointed to a cluster of plump red fruits hanging heavy on their vines. "They're ready when they're this deep color and just a little soft to the touch."

"Like this?" Ruby asked, gently squeezing one.

"Perfect," Amy praised. "Don't squeeze too hard or you'll look like you lost a fight with it."

Priscilla reached for a cucumber, her small fingers curling around the cool skin. "And this one?"

"Give it a little twist," Amy instructed, guiding Priscilla's hands. With a snap, the cucumber came free, and Priscilla's face lit up with pride.

"Good job, Priscilla!" Ruby said, giving her little sister an encouraging smile.

As they moved through the rows, Amy showed them how to spot the ripe bell peppers, their glossy skins a sign they were ready to be picked. They filled their baskets with the colorful harvest.

"Can we make a salad?" Ruby asked, holding up a carrot she had unearthed.

"We sure can," Amy said with a nod. "With all these fresh veggies, it'll be the best salad you've ever tasted."

"Yummy!" Priscilla cheered.

Amy led Ruby and Priscilla to a perfect picnic spot under a giant oak tree. She'd made a simple lunch for the others before mopping the floors and left it in the oven for them to serve themselves. She'd been married for almost a week now, and they would be headed to church the following morning. She couldn't help but think of how proud she'd be to be sitting with her family in the pews of the local church.

"Girls, how about we have ourselves a picnic right there?" she suggested, pointing to the shade.

"Picnic?" Priscilla's face lit up like the dawn, her little legs carrying her toward the oak as fast as they could manage.

Ruby's lips curved into a gentle smile, a rare sight that warmed Amy's heart. "That sounds nice," she said softly.

Amy smiled. "I'll go get the picnic basket I packed before I came outside." She hurried into the house and took the picnic basket off the table, happy to have time to spend with the little girls.

Under the canopy of the aged tree, Amy spread out a checkered blanket with corners worn from love and use. She unpacked the sandwiches and placed them alongside a large glass jar brimming with homemade lemonade. The sunlight filtered through the leaves, dappling the blanket in patterns of light and dark.

"Come sit," Amy beckoned, patting the blanket beside her.

The girls settled down, Ruby with her usual quiet grace and Priscilla with the unrestrained enthusiasm of youth. They each took a sandwich, the bread fresh and the filling hearty, just the way Amy knew would bring comfort.

"Try the lemonade. I squeezed the lemons this morning," Amy said, pouring the sweet, tangy liquid into tin cups.

"Yummy!" Priscilla declared, her voice bubbling with delight as she sipped.

"Good job, Amy," Ruby added, her approval more subdued but no less sincere.

As they ate, Amy watched the children with a tender gaze. "What do you girls like best about living on the ranch?" She was genuinely curious, wanting to know the souls of these little ones who had been entrusted to her care.

"I like the horses," Ruby confided, her eyes taking on a distant dreaminess. "They're strong and free."

Priscilla, crumbs dotting her chin, chimed in, "I climb trees!"

"Is that so?" Amy laughed, brushing away the stray bits of sandwich from Priscilla's face. "And what do you both dream of? For when you're grown?"

Ruby bit her lip, contemplating. "I'd like to be a teacher. To read lots of books and show others how."

"I want to fly like a bird!" Priscilla declared, spreading her arms wide.

"Those are beautiful dreams," Amy encouraged, her voice soft with sincerity. "And you can be anything you set your hearts on." She looked at Priscilla. "Except maybe a bird."

"Really?" Ruby seemed to search Amy's face for confirmation.

"Really," Amy affirmed. "You're part of a family that will always support you." Amy looked at the tree above them. "You know, my sister Gail married Mr. Carlson, and she can build anything. I think we should ask her to come visit and build us a treehouse, and we'll feed her cookies as payment."

"Could we?" Priscilla asked, looking excited.

"I'll talk to your papa about it, but I have a feeling he'll agree." Amy folded the checkered blanket with a smile, tucking it under her arm. "Let's head over to the stables now," she suggested.

Ruby and Priscilla scrambled to their feet, their energy renewed by the prospect of adventure. They trailed behind Amy, their small boots kicking up puffs of dust as they made their way across the ranch.

"Does your papa let you ride them?" Amy asked, her enthusiasm infectious as they approached the large wooden structure that housed the horses.

Ruby shook her head sadly. "He thinks girls are too delicate to ride horses."

Amy sighed. "A lot of men think that. But you know what?"

"What?" Ruby asked.

"I think the world is changing, and in another fifty years or so, girls are going to ride horses all the time!" At the stable door, she paused. "Horses need lots of care, but if you're gentle, they'll be your friends for life." Her words were like seeds planted in fertile soil, sowing curiosity and eagerness in Ruby and Priscilla's young minds.

"Can I really touch them?" Ruby's voice was a whisper of awe mixed with a hint of disbelief.

"Of course, you can." Amy's affirmation was warm and reassuring. She led them inside, where the scent of hay and leather mingled in the air.

"Hello, Jasper," Amy greeted the chestnut gelding nearest them, extending her hand slowly for him to sniff. The horse nuzzled her palm, his dark eyes gentle.

"See? Just like this." Amy picked up a brush from a nearby shelf and began to run it over Jasper's coat, her strokes rhythmic and sure. "Always go with the direction of their fur."

Priscilla watched, wide-eyed, then piped up, "My turn?"

"Here, use this smaller brush." Amy handed her a suitable tool for her tiny hands, watching as Priscilla mimicked her movements with childlike concentration.

Ruby took a brush too, her fingers gripping the handle as if it were a lifeline to a world she had only dared to dream of. Her strokes were tentative at first, but with each pass over the sleek coat, her confidence grew.

"Good job, Ruby," Amy encouraged. "You're a natural."

"Does he like it?" Ruby asked, her gaze never leaving the horse's flank.

"Very much," Amy replied, "Just like we enjoy a nice back rub."

They moved on to the hooves, and Amy showed the girls how to pick out the dirt and stones, explaining the importance of keeping the horses comfortable and healthy.

"Like checking for rocks in our shoes," Amy said, making sure the lesson was within their grasp.

"Yuck!" Priscilla exclaimed, giggling as a clump of mud dropped from the hoof. Yet her laughter was not one of disgust, but of discovery and joy in the messiness of life.

"Exactly, Priscilla," Amy laughed along, her heart swelling with pride at their quick learning. "It's all part of taking care of those who take care of us."

Amy led Ruby and Priscilla back to the house. "Did you girls enjoy that?" Amy asked, looking over her shoulder at the two young girls trailing behind her.

"Uh-huh," Priscilla nodded eagerly. "I never knew horses' hair could be so soft!"

"Me neither," Ruby chimed in, "and I liked picking their hooves. It was like finding treasure!"

Amy laughed. "Well, I'm glad to hear it. Now, let's get inside and start on supper. Who's hungry for chicken and dumplings?"

"Me!" both girls exclaimed, quickening their pace to match Amy's.

"And salad of course," Amy said, nodding to the veggies they'd picked that morning.

Amy tied an apron around her waist and set a large pot on the stove. She filled it with water and set it to boil while the girls watched, perched on wooden stools.

"Can we help?" Ruby offered.

"Of course," Amy replied. "Ruby, can you fetch the flour and baking powder? Priscilla, we need the chicken from the ice box."

The girls jumped into action, and soon the kitchen hummed with the harmonious sounds of collaboration. Amy skillfully deboned the chicken, her fingers deft and sure, while Ruby measured out the flour with a level of precision beyond her years. Priscilla watched Amy, absorbing every movement like a sponge.

"First, we'll make the dough for the dumplings," Amy instructed, guiding Ruby through the process. "Just like this, nice and gentle."

"Like petting the horses," Ruby mused, catching on quickly.

"Exactly," Amy smiled, impressed by the girl's connection.

Together, they rolled and cut the dough, dropping the pieces into the simmering broth.

"Smells good," Priscilla observed, her stomach growling in anticipation.

"Almost ready," Amy assured her, stirring the pot. "You two set the table?"

"Sure thing, Amy!" they said in unison, bouncing off their stools to lay out plates and silverware.

As the final touches to the meal were added—a pinch of salt here, a dash of pepper there—Amy stepped back, watching the girls work together. This was what family felt like, she realized. She couldn't have asked for a better way to end the day.

"Supper's ready!" Amy called, and the family gathered around the table, the enticing smell of chicken and dumplings drawing everyone in. They took their seats, passing bowls and sharing stories of the day, the laughter and chatter melding into the melody of ranch life. Amy looked around, her heart full. This was home, and these were the moments she would cherish forever.

Chapter Seven

Amy sat on the edge of the bed, her hands clasped together, waiting for the perfect moment to speak. Tim was washing up, his movements slow and deliberate, the sound of water splashing a gentle rhythm in the quiet room.

"Tim?" Amy said as he dried his hands and turned toward her.

"Sure, what is it?" Tim replied, a smile tugging at the corners of his mouth as he sat down beside her. He was thrilled with their arrangement so far. The children were doing well, and she was a better cook than anyone he'd ever known.

"I've been thinking about asking my sister Gail to build a treehouse for the kids," she said, her gaze fixed on his face to gauge his reaction. "She's got magic hands for that sort of work. Thought maybe I could pay her in cookies or such since she'd rather climb trees than be stuck by a stove."

"Sounds fair enough." Tim chuckled. "But you know Gail married Max, the one who owns the restaurant and hotel in town? You might find yourself cooking there for a day or two. Max won't be able to spare Gail for long, and that would be a good way of paying them back. With the way you cook, he'll never want to let you leave."

Amy bit her lip, considering this, before nodding resolutely. "Then that's what I'll do. I'm sure Gail will be thrilled to have a couple of days doing what she does best. She's a good cook, but she hates it so much! I think it would be a fair trade for the littles to have a place to play, don't you think?"

"Can't argue with that," he agreed, leaning back against the headboard and pulling her close.

Their conversation meandered through plans and dreams. The night deepened around them, but inside their little world, time seemed to stand still.

Tim's hand found hers, his touch warm and steady. His fingers traced delicate patterns on the back of her hand, sending shivers up her spine. She leaned into him, her breath catching as his other hand brushed a stray lock of hair from her face, tucking it behind her ear.

"Tim..." she whispered, her heart fluttering like the wings of a trapped bird.

"Shh," he murmured, his lips finding hers in the darkness. Their kiss was gentle at first, testing, exploring, but as the seconds slipped away, it grew deeper, hungrier.

The rest of the world fell away. It was just the two of them, wrapped in each other's arms, the steady beat of their hearts echoing through the silence of the night. They moved together, desire making them hungry for one another.

AMY PADDED SOFTLY THROUGH the still house. Sunday's early light crept through the windows. She moved with practiced quietness, laying out the neatly pressed garments at the foot of each bed. George's shirt and trousers were easy, but her fingers lingered on the fabric of Beatrice's dress, its plain cut a stark contrast to what a young lady might desire. A gentle sigh escaped her lips—Beatrice deserved something finer, something that would let the girl shine.

"Got to make some proper dresses for Bea," Amy murmured to herself, envisioning soft laces and satins.

With the clothing sorted, she tiptoed to the kitchen. The comforting ritual of cooking filled her with a sense of purpose and peace. First, she cracked eggs into a bowl, whisking them with a dash of salt before pouring them into the sizzling pan. Next came the toast, each slice crisping to golden perfection under her watchful eye. She hummed a tune, lost in the rhythm of assembling sandwiches packed with the fluffy eggs and savory sausage.

"Smells like heaven in here," Tim's voice broke the morning's quiet as he emerged, rubbing sleep from his eyes.

"Morning, " Amy greeted him with a smile, placing a steaming mug of coffee on the table. "Thought we'd start the day right."

"Can't argue with that," Tim said, taking a seat and reaching for a sandwich. His appreciative grin was all the thanks she needed.

"Sunday best is all laid out for the kids," she added, pouring herself a cup of coffee and joining him.

"Beatrice too?" Tim asked between bites. "She's not always the best behaved at church these days."

"Especially Beatrice," Amy replied. "Though I think she needs something new, something with a touch of grace."

"Sounds like a plan," Tim agreed, nodding. "You seem to know what they all need."

Their conversation flowed as easily as the coffee they shared, a simple joy found in the quiet moments of the morning.

The children gathered for breakfast. "George, you're hogging all the sandwiches. If you take three then I don't get one!" Beatrice's voice was particularly shrill as she glared at her brother.

"Am not!" George protested with a scowl. "Just eat your eggs, Beatrice."

Amy watched them, her heart sinking a little. The balance between stepmother and disciplinarian was a tightrope she walked daily. She set down her sandwich, untouched, and attempted to broker peace. "Now, let's share nicely. There's plenty for everyone."

"Doesn't feel like it," Beatrice muttered, glaring at her brother before snatching a sandwich from his plate.

"Enough, Beatrice." Amy's voice was firm. She caught George's eye, hoping he would let the matter drop.

George sighed. "This isn't going to be enough, and my stomach will growl all through church."

"Here, take mine. I can make another," Amy said, giving him an encouraging smile.

The meal continued with less bickering but an undercurrent of tension that had Amy worrying about what her first church service with her family would be like.

After breakfast, Tim stepped outside to hitch up the wagon. Amy followed, smoothing down her simple dress, her hands trembling. She couldn't believe how nervous she was about going to church in her new community.

"Ready?" Tim called over his shoulder, the lines around his eyes crinkling as he smiled reassuringly at her.

"Guess I have to be," Amy replied, mustering a brave front. Her palms felt clammy against the fabric of her skirt.

"Hey, it's just church," Tim chuckled. "And after today, it'll just be another Sunday routine."

"Hope so," she whispered, more to herself than to him.

"Look at it this way," Tim said as he took the reins and gave her a sidelong glance, "it's a fine day for introductions."

"Sure is," Amy agreed, the optimism in Tim's tone infectious. She settled into the seat beside him, taking comfort in the warmth of his presence. The children all climbed into the back of the wagon, and Amy sensed there was still friction between George and Beatrice.

Amy stepped down from the wagon in front of the church, her heart lightening at the sight of friendly faces. Elizabeth's blond hair glimmered in the sunlight, and Susan's warm smile beckoned her closer.

"Elizabeth! Susan!" Amy exclaimed, rushing over to embrace them both. "It's so good to see you."

"Look at you, a breath of fresh air," Elizabeth said with a chuckle, her eyes crinkling at the corners.

"Welcome to the community, Amy," Susan added, her voice rich with maternal warmth.

Their familiar banter helped settle Amy's nerves. And then she saw Gail, her sister, standing a little apart, her gaze lingering on the oak trees that dotted the churchyard.

"Gail!" Amy called out, hurrying toward her. "I've been dreaming of a treehouse for the children. You think you could build one?"

Gail turned, her face lighting up with enthusiasm. "Treehouse? I'd love to! But, Amy, I won't take cookies as payment this time."

"Deal," Amy laughed. "How about a day of cooking at the restaurant instead?"

"Perfect! I'm tired of cooking anyway, and we both know you're a much better cook than I am." Gail grinned, clapping her hands together in excitement.

As they chatted about the treehouse, Amy's eyes wandered to the front steps of the church where Hannah stood, her arms wrapped around herself in a self-embrace, speaking earnestly with Amos, the pastor.

"Excuse me, Gail," Amy said, her curiosity piqued. She made her way to her younger sister, whose presence in such a holy place seemed as out of character as a fish climbing a tree.

"Hannah?" Amy approached cautiously. "What brings you here?"

Hannah turned, a small, almost shy smile playing on her lips. "Oh, Amy, you wouldn't believe it. Amos and I, we...we got married."

"Married?" Amy blinked, taken aback by the revelation. "But you and church..."

"He wasn't even there to meet a woman. He was only there to perform weddings, but I saw him, and well..." Hannah said, her eyes softening as she glanced at Amos.

"Congratulations," Amy managed, though a knot of concern formed in her stomach. Hannah and faith had always been like oil and water. Could such a union truly last?

"Thank you, Amy," Hannah replied. "I hope you'll support us."

"Of course, Hannah," Amy assured her, though the doubt lingered like a stubborn shadow. Attraction was powerful, but was it enough to bridge the gap between a skeptic and a pastor? Only time would tell.

The sermon was well underway, the pastor's voice a gentle hum in the background when Amy caught movement out of the corner of her eye. She turned just in time to see Beatrice's foot connect with George's shin, not with the playful tap of siblings in silent disagreement, but with the sharpness of pent-up frustration. George's yelp sliced through the pastor's words, and silence fell like a heavy curtain over the congregation.

Amy felt a blush warm her cheeks as heads swiveled their way, eyes filled with curious disapproval. She stood swiftly, skirts rustling softly against the pew. With a firm but gentle grip, she took Beatrice's hand, whispering words meant to soothe and scold all at once. "Now, Beatrice, you know that's no way to act in the Lord's house."

"Sorry," Beatrice muttered, not meeting Amy's gaze as they made their way down the aisle.

"Let's step outside for some fresh air," Amy suggested, her tone light despite the weight of embarrassment settled on her shoulders. They slipped out the church door and into the heat of the Texas sun.

"Church is a place of peace, Bea," Amy said. "We need to show respect, even when we're feeling cross."

Beatrice scuffed her shoe against the dirt, her defiance wilting under Amy's kind gaze. "I know, I just...I don't like it here without Ma," she whispered, her voice quivering like leaves in a breeze. "Pa has been letting me stay home for months, but when I saw you'd laid out a dress for me, I knew I had to come."

Amy rested her hands gently on the girl's shoulders. "I understand. Truly I do," she said with a warmth that reached straight into Beatrice's stormy heart. "But I'm here for you, and I promise, together we'll find a way through this."

Amy fiddled with the brim of her bonnet, watching as the last of the congregation filed out of the church. She caught sight of Susan Dailey. Taking in a deep breath, Amy approached her.

"Mrs. Dailey?" Amy's voice was hesitant yet hopeful.

Susan turned, her smile as welcoming as the warm bread she often baked. "Yes, Amy. How are you settling in?"

"Quite well, thank you," Amy replied. "But I—I wonder if I might ask for some advice."

"Of course, dear." Susan's eyebrows lifted in a gesture of attentive concern.

"It's about Beatrice. She...She seems to be profoundly sad, and I'm having a hard time getting through to her." Amy's fingers twisted the fabric of her skirt. "I thought maybe, since you've been a stepmother..." Amy shook her head. "It's so hard to know what the right thing is to do."

"Ah." Understanding dawned on Susan's face. "These things take time. And love, plenty of love. Why don't you and Tim come over for supper tonight? We can talk more then."

"Really?" A budding hope took root in Amy's chest.

"Really. It's nothing fancy, but we Daileys believe there's no trouble too big that it can't be soothed by good company and a hearty meal."

"Thank you." Amy's gratitude was clear. "We'll be there."

"Good, it's settled then!" Susan declared before waving off to another parishioner.

Amy felt a touch lighter as she walked back to where Tim was hitching up the wagon, ready to navigate the bumpy roads—and relationships—of their newfound life together.

Chapter Eight

Amy tied her apron around her waist and set to work in the warm kitchen. The scent of roasting chicken filled the small homestead, a comforting aroma that spoke of family gatherings and quiet afternoons. With practiced hands, she rolled out pastry dough for the blackberry pies, her thoughts drifting to the Daileys' kindness.

"George, Beatrice," she called over her shoulder, "I need you two to keep an eye on the little ones tonight."

George leaned against the kitchen doorframe. "We'll manage," he said.

Beatrice nodded, though her lips were a thin line of reluctance. "Of course," she replied.

Tim ambled into the kitchen, his hat in hand. He ruffled George's hair, earning a scowl from the boy. "Now, I expect you both to do your share. No roughhousing inside the house." His voice was firm but gentle.

Amy slid the first pie into the oven and then turned to face the children, her expression earnest. "And no fussing," she added, looking directly at Beatrice, who held her chin up defiantly.

"Supper's on the stove," Amy continued. "Make sure everyone eats together."

"Can we have pie too?" one of the younger ones piped up from behind Beatrice, eyes wide with hope.

"Only if there's some left when we get back," Tim answered with a chuckle, winking at Amy.

Amy shook her head. "I made three. One for here and two to take with us. We're trusting you two. We'll be back after supper at the Daileys.'"

"Go on, then," George urged. "We won't burn the place down."

"Or each other," Beatrice muttered under her breath, but a ghost of a smile flickered across her face.

"Thank you," Amy said. She placed the other pies in the oven and glanced at Tim. Oh, how she hoped that the Daileys would have good advice for dealing with Beatrice.

Amy and Tim approached the Dailey homestead, the lingering guilt in Amy's heart warring with a flutter of anticipation. Tim reached for her hand, giving it an encouraging squeeze, his gaze softening as they neared the porch where Susan stood waiting, an embodiment of hospitality.

"Welcome!" Susan opened the door wide and invited Amy and Tim inside. "We're glad to have you both."

"Thank you for having us," Amy replied. "It's nice to get out, just the two of us."

"Come on in," Susan said, ushering them into the parlor with a motherly touch. "I remember what it's like, needing a bit of grown-up time." She laughed softly, settling Amy onto a plush settee. "When I married David, his little ones were simply other versions of the siblings I'd left behind in Massachusetts, and those siblings are the main reason I left."

"Your siblings are legendary with their pranks." Amy said.

Susan shook her head. "Not in a good way at all, though. So here's what I think I would do with a sullen teenage girl."

Amy listened intently, feeling a bond form as Susan shared her story, the kind that only women who've walked similar paths could understand.

Meanwhile, David's chuckle floated from the adjoining room, where he and Tim had begun to converse. "So, Tim," David's voice was as relaxed as his posture against the mantle, "how's ranching treating you?"

"Better now with summer," Tim admitted, his own tension easing under the spell of David's easy nature. "And your horses? How's that new stallion faring?"

"Strong-willed like I've never seen," David confessed, "but there's no better feeling than when you finally reach an understanding with horses like him."

Amy could hear the men sharing a hearty laugh, and she smiled to herself, grateful for this unexpected kinship blooming between their families. As Susan continued to recount her early days of marriage, offering wisdom wrapped in kindness, Amy felt the last threads of unease slip away, replaced by a growing sense of camaraderie and hope for the future.

Amy perched on the edge of the settee, her hands clasped in her lap, while Susan's laughter filled the parlor. The scent of blackberry pie lingered, a sweet reminder of Amy's gratitude for this visit.

"Thank you so much for the pies," Susan said. "My kids will have them gone by breakfast."

Amy chuckled. "I just hope they taste as good as they smell."

"Trust me, with hands like yours? They're divine," Susan assured her. "From what I heard from Elizabeth, your pies are nothing less than culinary masterpieces."

From the other room, David's hearty guffaw punctuated the conversation. "Tim, you ever seen a stallion try to court a mare? I think that stallion of mine's got ideas above his station!"

"Sounds like quite the spectacle!" Tim's voice carried a lightheartedness Amy had never heard from him.

Susan leaned forward, her eyes locking onto Amy's with an understanding that bridged the space between them. "Blending a family is like kneading dough. You push and fold, and sometimes you swear it won't come together. But then, it does. Becomes something stronger. And it's all right if it's messy at first. Mine started as just his, and then we had some of ours. None of them think of themselves as half-siblings though. They're all just brothers and sisters. Of course, one of my stepsons married one of my sisters, so that wasn't exactly normal."

"Alice was telling us that!" Amy said, the corners of her mouth twitching upwards.

"I didn't even recognize her because she was so little when I left Massachusetts, and we haven't made a trip back."

Amy watched Susan as the woman shared a funny story about her siblings. Across the room, Tim leaned against the mantelpiece, hat in hand, nodding as David shared another one of his ranch anecdotes.

"Beatrice is...she's been a challenge," Amy admitted. "She misses her mother something fierce, and I think she sees me as the enemy. I've tried to tell her that I'm not there to take her mother's place, but she doesn't seem to believe me."

Susan's brow furrowed with empathy. "Girls at that age can be thorny, like rose bushes. But even roses need tending to bloom."

"Thorny is one word for it," Amy said.

"David and I, we've been through our share of troubles," Susan continued. "When it comes to young ladies, you've got to find that spot between firm ground and gentle rain."

"Sounds easier said than done," Amy replied, her gaze drifting to Tim.

"Perhaps," Susan agreed. "Give Beatrice time. Listen more than you speak. And when you do speak, let it be with kindness—even when it feels like pouring sugar on a cactus."

"I feel like I already do that, but I'll try a little harder. Beatrice really needs dresses that don't make her look like a little girl. Maybe we can sew a few dresses together, and that will help her warm up to me," Amy said.

"Trust me, Amy," Susan added. "In time, she'll see your heart. And if you ever need to talk or just escape for a spell, our door's always open."

"Thank you," Amy said, her voice steady for the first time that evening. "Both of you."

"Family isn't just blood," Susan said, her eyes sparkling with sincerity. "It's the people who stand by you, come what may."

Amy folded her hands together, warmth blossoming in her chest as she glanced over at Susan. "I can't tell you how much this means to us," she said.

Susan waved off the thanks with a chuckle. "Oh, hush now. What are neighbors for? Besides, I think we all need each other."

Timothy nodded from across the room, where he leaned against the mantle. "I must admit, I've learned more about horses and family in one evening than I have in years. Thank you, David."

"Shoot, Tim," David replied with a wry grin. "You'll be outdoing me on the ranch before long. Just remember, it's all about balance—whether you're breaking a stallion or raising a family."

"Balance and patience," Amy mused aloud. "Sounds like the recipe for a happy home."

"Exactly," Susan agreed. "And don't forget a dollop of love. It covers a multitude of sins."

"Speaking of love," David chimed in, "I do believe that's what got us all sitting here tonight, isn't it? Love for our families and the land we call home."

"True enough," Timothy said, nodding. "It's good to find friends who become like family."

"And I have a feeling we're going to be exactly that to each other!" David raised his glass, and the others followed suit.

Later, Susan set down her empty teacup with a soft clink. "Amy, your blackberry pie tonight was divine. I must know your secret."

"Ah, it's in the berries," Amy replied, tucking a stray lock of hair behind her ear. "Picked fresh this afternoon with the two sweetest little helpers in the world—Ruby and Priscilla." She leaned closer, as if to share a treasured secret. "And a spoonful of honey in the crust—works wonders."

"Really?" Susan asked. "I've never tried that. My pies are good, but yours..." She shook her head in appreciation. "They're something special."

"Thank you. But I'm certain your pies are just as good," Amy said. "Besides, when you bake with love, you can taste it in every bite."

"Maybe that's what I need to focus on—baking with an extra dash of love."

As they stood, Amy helped clear the small table of their teacups, feeling a sense of comfort in the domestic ritual. The evening had helped her to understand there was no true right way to deal with the situation. But it had to be handled with both patience and love.

"Let's get you home before the stars claim the night," Susan suggested, guiding Amy toward the front door where Tim stood waiting, hat in hand.

"Thank you for everything, Susan. For the advice...and for listening." Amy's voice carried the weight of her gratitude.

"Anytime, dear," Susan assured her. "Remember, we're just a stone's throw away."

Tim offered his arm to Amy, and together they stepped out into the cool embrace of the Texas night. The sky, a vast expanse of velvet dotted with twinkling stars, seemed to echo the boundless opportunities before them.

"Beatrice may be a tough nut to crack," Tim said quietly, "but we'll find a way to her heart."

"Like Susan said, 'Love and patience,'" Amy mused, her resolve hardening.

"Sounds like a plan," Tim agreed, his demeanor hopeful under the moon's gentle glow. "We'll reach her, one way or another."

Chapter Nine

The afternoon sun cast a golden glow over the homestead as Amy rounded up her little flock with an announcement that had everyone's eyes sparkling. "Girls, we need to get ready—we're heading to town for new dresses!"

Ruby's shy smile peeked out from behind a curtain of hair, and Priscilla's tiny feet danced a jig on the wooden floorboards. Beatrice, however, bore the air of someone bestowed a rare gift. "Two for me?" she verified, voice lilting with a mix of disbelief and delight.

"Yes," confirmed Amy, tying on her bonnet. "The little girls still have dresses they can wear. Nothing you have fits anymore!"

As they made their way to the wagon, Beatrice practically floated to her seat beside Amy, each step a dance of anticipation. The wagon creaked under their weight, the horses snorting softly, ready to tread the familiar path to town.

"Ruffles would be so pretty," mused Beatrice. "And maybe some lace right here..." She gestured delicately around her neck and wrists, her imagination painting elaborate garments in the air before them.

Amy chuckled, reining in both the horses and Beatrice's fanciful ideas with gentle firmness. "We can put lace around your collar and sleeves, but remember, we need dresses for everyday life not big dance parties."

"Of course, Amy," Beatrice conceded with a playful roll of her eyes.

The bell above the store door jingled, heralding the arrival of Amy and her lively entourage. The shop's cozy interior was lined with bolts of fabric. Amy approached the counter, the reticule in her hand giving her the money she needed for her shopping.

"Goodness," she murmured, thumbing through the folded bills Tim had entrusted to her care. Her brows knit together. This was more money than she'd seen in a long while, enough to make her head spin like a top.

"Is something wrong, Amy?" Beatrice asked, peering at Amy.

Amy hesitated, then shook her head, laughing softly at her own surprise. "It's just...well, I didn't expect so much."

"Pa said it's for groceries too," Beatrice said. "He knows we eat a lot."

"Yes, we do," Amy agreed with a smile. "Well, let's see about those fabrics, shall we?"

Ruby, quiet as a mouse but with eyes wide as saucers, pointed to a bolt of vibrant red cloth. "Like roses," she whispered.

"More like rubies, don't you think?" Amy asked, hugging the girl with one arm.

"Pink!" Priscilla declared. "Pink like... like candy!"

"Then pink it shall be," Amy announced, her heart warmed by their simple joys. Beatrice, meanwhile, had wandered to a table laden with yard goods.

As Amy helped the girls pick out the perfect prints—a dainty floral for Ruby and playful polka dots for Priscilla—she couldn't help but think how each fabric seemed to capture the girls' personalities.

"Found anything you fancy, Beatrice?" asked Amy, glancing over at the eldest girl.

"Maybe," Beatrice replied, the ghost of a smile on her face as she set the fabric aside. "But let's get the little ones sorted first."

"All right then," Amy agreed, herding the excited children to the counter so they could put them down and continue shopping. As the clerk started their order, Amy realized that the excursion had been successful, with all three girls excited that they were getting exactly what they wanted.

Beatrice drifted back to the table she had abandoned earlier, her gaze now settled on two bolts of fabric. The first was a sky blue adorned with delicate white flowers, and the second, a vibrant green as fresh as new leaves unfurling under the morning sun.

"Blue for the sky," Beatrice murmured, almost to herself, "and green for the fields." She looked up at Amy with a rare flicker of excitement in her eyes. "I like these."

Amy beamed at her, thrilled at the girl's budding enthusiasm "Those are beautiful choices, Beatrice. They'll suit you perfectly."

With the younger girls' choices bundled and set aside, it was Amy's turn to peruse the shelves. Her hands found a bolt of plain white fabric, smooth and cool to the touch—perfect for a nightgown to replace the one she'd worn threadbare. She would also be sure to get enough to make aprons for all three of the girls.

She thought she'd surprise the girls with them as soon as all three were done.

Amy's fingers lingered on a roll of fabric that seemed to call out to her. It was a lovely floral print, a cascade of wildflowers that danced across a soft cream background. It was just the sort of dress she could wear when the weather turned fair, maybe to the Sunday service or to any summer parties.

"This one's for me," she said, a hint of dreaminess in her voice. Never before had she been given the opportunity to choose her own fabric for a dress. She was used to wearing the hand-me-downs all of the children in the foundling home had worn.

"Very pretty," Beatrice acknowledged. "You'll look nice in it."

"Thank you, Beatrice." Amy smiled. "Now, let's get these home so we can start creating."

"Can't wait," Beatrice replied, seeming to be genuinely happy to be shopping with Amy and her sisters.

Amy's arms brimmed with bolts of fabric as she approached the counter, her charges trailing behind her, each of them with full arms.

The clerk, a portly man with a waxed mustache, watched with a bemused expression as they unloaded their bounty. Ruby and Priscilla giggled while piling on buttons and spools of thread, each one chosen with care.

"Will that be all, Mrs. Stockwell?" the clerk asked, his eyes darting from the mountainous stack to Amy's face.

"Just about," Amy replied. "We'll need to pick up some provisions for the week ahead."

The girls set to work once more, this time navigating the narrow aisles lined with jars of preserves, sacks of flour, and tins of tea. Beatrice's nose scrunched as she deliberated between two bags of oats, finally choosing the one that seemed fuller.

"Can't forget Mr. Stockwell's favorite molasses," Amy reminded them, reaching for the sticky jug. "And some of these dried apples—they'll bake up nice."

"Priscilla loves apple pie," Ruby chimed in.

"Then apple pie it shall be," Amy decided, adding the fruit to their growing pile.

As the last can of beans clinked onto the counter, Amy's gaze fell upon a basket of soft woolen yarns, their colors rich and inviting. She hesitated only a moment before selecting skeins in hues of charcoal and oatmeal.

"Going to knit some warmth into those boys' come winter," she said with a determined nod, picturing George and Tim out on the chilly range, their feet snug in the socks she'd craft by the firelight.

"George will like that," Beatrice observed, a rare note of affection in her voice for her brother.

"Tim too," Amy agreed, smiling at the thought of the men's surprise when they slipped their feet into her handiwork.

"All right then," the clerk announced, tallying up their goods. "That should do it, unless you've got a hankering for anything else."

Amy shook her head, content with their haul. "This will see us through just fine."

"Very good, Mrs. Stockwell." He offered a nod, appreciative of her decisiveness.

"Come on, girls," Amy beckoned, ready to return home and start on their sewing adventures. "Let's get these things back to the wagon."

"Can we help make the pie?" Priscilla asked, her eyes wide with hope.

"Of course," Amy assured her, her heart swelling with the simple joy of these shared moments.

Amy lingered a moment longer than the others, her gaze caught by the gleam of polished metal in the corner. There was a sewing machine. She'd seen such contraptions in passing—marvels of the modern age that promised to transform the labor of needle and thread into something swift and effortless.

"Never touched one before," she mused aloud, her fingers tracing the contours of the cool metal and intricate gears. It was a beautiful piece, solid and promising.

"Looks complicated," murmured Ruby from behind her, clutching her chosen red fabric to her chest.

"Perhaps, but think of the time it would save," Amy replied, her voice tinged with a mix of awe and practicality. Then she remembered Tim's money was meant for necessities, not luxuries. With a gentle pat on the machine's side, she turned away, her thoughts already flipping through patterns and meals as she herded the girls out of the store.

"Let's get these treasures loaded up," she said brightly.

The ride home was filled with chatter about the dresses they would make and the pies they would bake. But once they arrived, Beatrice's sudden request surprised Amy.

"May I go for a walk?" Beatrice asked, her voice quieter than usual.

"Alone?" Amy's brows raised in surprise. The girl had been stuck to her side like glue since their arrival at the store.

"Need some air," came Beatrice's simple reply, her eyes not quite meeting Amy's.

"All right then," Amy conceded, her curiosity piqued but her tone supportive. "But don't wander too far. Supper won't wait for any young lady."

"Promise," Beatrice said and, with a quick hitch of her skirt, she was off, leaving Amy to watch her go, a small smile playing on her lips.

Amy spread the soft pink fabric across the worn wooden table, the gleam in Priscilla's eyes reflecting the gentle hue. The little girl clapped her hands with unbridled excitement.

"It's so pretty!" Priscilla exclaimed.

"Yes, it'll make a fine dress for you," Amy replied, measuring and snipping with practiced ease, her heart buoyant amidst the flutters of cotton.

"Can we add some fairy wings to it to make me fly?" Priscilla asked.

"We won't attach them to the dress, but I'll make some fairy wings," Amy chuckled, envisioning Priscilla twirling in her new dress.

"Ruffles!" Ruby chimed in, bouncing on her toes. "Lots and lots!"

"Ruffles it is," Amy agreed, nodding at the eager child. "This will be a church dress, so ruffles are necessary!"

As if summoned by Amy's musings, Beatrice reappeared, her face flushed from the walk and looking excited. She hovered near the table, watching Amy's hands move.

"I want my dress with...with a train!" Beatrice declared.

"Trains are lovely," Amy said, placing the scissors down, "but not very practical for every day. You know how muddy it can get."

"Then maybe just..." Beatrice trailed off, biting her lip in thought.

"Here," Amy offered, rummaging through a modest pile of patterns, "these are what I have. But none quite match your grand ideas."

Beatrice's nose wrinkled in mild frustration before a spark lit up her features. "Wait here!" she instructed, dashing away before anyone could utter a word. Curiosity bubbled within Amy as she continued pinning the fabric for Priscilla's dress.

Moments later, Beatrice returned, arms straining beneath the weight of a dusty crate.

"Mother's patterns," Beatrice said, her voice softer. "She loved making dresses."

"Your mother had exquisite taste," Amy observed, peering into the crate.

Together they sifted through the designs, the air tinged with memories and muted hope. Beatrice's finger halted on an elaborate drawing, her expression brightening.

"This one," she said, laying the paper pattern atop the others. "It looks like my mother's favorite dress, but my colors will be different."

"Of course," Amy smiled, "we can start on yours after we finish with Priscilla's."

"Thank you, Amy," Beatrice murmured with a smile.

"Always," Amy replied. She felt as if she and Beatrice had a true breakthrough.

AMY TRACED THE DELICATE lines of the sewing pattern with her finger. Beatrice beamed down at the intricate sketch on the table—a high-waisted dress with just the right amount of frill for a young lady of twelve.

"Are you sure?" Amy asked, knowing full well the joy dancing in Beatrice's eyes.

"It's perfect," Beatrice said. "Just like she would have made."

"Priscilla's dress is already laid out. Mind if I stitch hers up first?" Amy asked, wishing she could do them all at the same time. "If you want to help sew, it will be done much faster."

"I'll help," Beatrice agreed.

The day waned as Amy tucked Priscilla's dress under her arm and moved toward the oven. The scent of baking bread wafted through the room, mingling with the earthy aroma of stewing herbs. She slid the supper inside.

The front door creaked open. George ambled in, his grin wide enough to split his face in two, while Tim followed, muscles straining against the bulk of something hidden from view.

"Look what we have here," George announced.

Together, they heaved their surprise onto the wooden floor—a sewing machine, sleek and gleaming even in the dimming light. The very one Amy had admired in town but dared not dream of owning.

"Is this..." Her words faltered, disbelief etching her features as she turned to Beatrice, who stood a little straighter, a conspiratorial glint in her eye.

"I knew you wanted it but wouldn't buy it for yourself." Beatrice's voice held a note of mischief. "Besides, we'll all get dresses faster this way."

Amy's heart swelled, the corners of her mouth lifting in a smile. Just when she'd started to wonder if she and Beatrice would ever see eye to eye...

Amy's hands trembled as she reached out to touch the sewing machine, her fingers grazing over the glossy black surface etched with delicate gold filigree.

"Beatrice," Amy said, her voice a mixture of gratitude and wonder. She turned to the young girl who stood watching her, an impish smile playing on her lips.

With a couple of quick strides, Amy closed the distance between them and wrapped Beatrice in a heartfelt embrace. "This is exactly what I need," she whispered, her words muffled by Beatrice's hair.

"Thought you'd say that," Beatrice replied, her arms returning the hug with equal fervor.

"Aren't you going to thank Pa?" George asked.

"Of course," Amy said, pulling back to look at both men standing there, their faces flushed from the effort of carrying the heavy machine—and perhaps from the satisfaction of their good deed.

"Thank you, both of you," she added, directing her gaze toward Tim, who nodded.

"Can't wait to see what magic you'll whip up with this thing," Tim said.

"So much magic," Amy agreed, her mind already racing with the possibilities now laid open before her. "First up, Priscilla's dress!"

"Then mine," Beatrice piped up.

"Then yours," Amy confirmed.

Chapter Ten

Amy's laughter mingled with the soft strums of the guitar as Tim plucked at the strings, his fingers dancing over the fretboard with a practiced ease. They sat together on the wooden porch of their ranch house. Shadows flickered across Tim's features, lending a tender roughness to his smile that made Amy's heart skip.

"Tim, this is perfect," she whispered.

"Only the best for my lady," he replied, setting the guitar aside and reaching across the small table to squeeze her hand.

They shared a meal of smoked brisket and fresh vegetables from the garden.

WHEN THE SUN ROSE THE following morning, Amy was already in the kitchen. She moved with purpose, cracking eggs and whisking them into a fluffy yellow sea—a skill she had honed since childhood. The sizzle of bacon joined the chorus of morning sounds, and the aroma of strong coffee filled the air.

"Morning," Tim greeted, wrapping his arms around Amy's waist from behind and kissing her cheek. His children trailed behind him like sleepy ducklings, their eyes brightening at the sight of breakfast.

"Good morning," Amy said, sliding a heaping plate onto the worn wooden table. "Hope y'all are hungry."

"Smells delicious, Amy," Tim said, taking his seat. The children gathered eagerly, and Tim was pleased it was no longer a chore to coax the children to eat. Amy had seen to that.

"Thanks to you, we'll never go hungry again," Priscilla said.

After the morning meal had settled and the clatter of dishes subsided, Amy found Tim on the porch, a look of contentment on his face as he surveyed the expanse of their land. She stepped out, the wooden boards creaking gently under her feet, and leaned against the railing beside him.

"Everything you do around here...it's more than I could have asked for," Tim said, turning toward her. "You've made this place alive again, Amy. It feels like a real home."

Amy blushed at his words. "I'm just doing what feels right," she replied modestly. "Seeing you and the kids happy—that's what matters to me."

Tim reached out, his hand brushing hers. "Well, we are. More than you know," he assured her.

"Tim, why don't we take the kids down to the creek later? We could have a picnic supper after your work is done," she suggested, her eyes bright with the thought. "They could swim, and we could all relax together."

"Sounds perfect," Tim agreed, his face lighting up at the prospect. "It'll be good to step away from the chores for a while and just enjoy each other's company."

"Great! I'll get everything ready." Amy's spirit lifted at the plan, envisioning the joy on the children's faces, the warm water, and the shared moments yet to come.

"Thank you," Tim said, and the simple words carried a world of meaning. They stood side by side looking forward to the hours ahead.

Amy bustled around the kitchen, her apron dusted with flour as she reached for the woven picnic basket. She tucked in sandwiches wrapped in brown paper—thick slices of ham and cheese nestled between hearty bread.

"George, can you fetch the blanket from the chest?" Amy called, her voice filled with warmth. The young boy scampered off, eager to help.

"Got it, Amy!" he exclaimed, returning with a woolen blanket.

"Perfect," she smiled, placing it atop the basket. "Let's head to the creek."

The sun dipped low, staining the sky in shades of pink and orange. Amy led them to a shaded spot by the gurgling creek, its waters whispering promises of respite from the afternoon heat.

"Okay, you little fish," Amy chuckled. "Let's get you ready to swim."

With gentle hands, she helped them out of their clothes, leaving them in their cotton undergarments, which would pass just fine for swimming attire.

"Into the water you go, but stay where I can see you," Amy instructed, her eyes sparkling with mirth as the children dashed into the creek.

"Be careful, Priscilla. I don't want you going too deep!" she called after the youngest, who nodded vigorously before joining her siblings.

Tim spread the checkered blanket with a practiced flick of his wrists, settling it on the grassy bank of the creek. The soft murmur of water mixed with children's laughter, and Amy was thrilled her plan had made the children so happy.

"Look at them," Amy said. "They're like little ducks, aren't they?"

"Sure are," Tim agreed, his gaze softening as he watched them. He passed Amy a sandwich, their fingers brushing briefly. A spark of warmth surged between them, unspoken but deeply felt.

"Speaking of building things," Amy began, pausing to take a bite of her sandwich, "Gail's coming over to build that treehouse I mentioned. I told her she could start Thursday."

"Is that so?" Tim raised an eyebrow, a smile playing on his lips. "Well, then I think I'll swing by the sawmill Wednesday. Pick up all the wood Gail will need."

"Good thinking." Amy nodded, her heart swelling at the thought of their future plans—a sturdy treehouse for the children, and perhaps one day, more little feet pattering about. "We need a few more kids to play in it."

"More kids, huh?" Tim chuckled, leaning back on his hands and looking up at the sky. "Sure, why not? A dozen or so should do."

"Only a dozen?" Amy teased, nudging him gently with her elbow.

"Give or take," he replied, his laughter mingling with hers.

Amy spotted a solitary figure perched on a rock at the edge of the creek— Beatrice, her knees hugged to her chest, watching the others with a distant gaze.

"Beatrice?" Amy called softly. She excused herself from Tim's side and approached the young lady. "Mind if I sit with you for a spell?"

Beatrice shrugged. Amy took it as invitation enough and settled beside her, leaving a respectful space between them.

"Beautiful evening, isn't it?" Amy asked, her voice gentle. "The water looks inviting. You don't want to swim?"

"No, thanks." Beatrice's reply was short, her eyes fixed on the rippling surface.

"All right." Amy nodded. "You know, I used to love collecting pretty stones by the creek when I was your age. Ever try that?"

"Sometimes," Beatrice murmured.

"Found any treasures today?" Amy asked.

"Maybe." A hint of pride laced Beatrice's words, and she pulled a small, smooth stone from her pocket.

"That's a real beauty," Amy admired honestly.

"Tell me, do you enjoy stories?" Amy asked, tilting her head curiously. "I'm rather fond of them myself."

Beatrice hesitated, then nodded. "I like books. Ma used to read to me."

"Is that so?" A soft smile graced Amy's lips. "What sort of tales did your ma favor?"

"Adventures. And ones with horses." The words tumbled out more freely now.

"Have you ever ridden?" Amy's question held a spark of hope. This was familiar ground for her, too.

"Ma taught me." Pride laced her voice, a sliver of warmth breaking through.

"Would you teach me about your favorite spots to ride around here?" Amy asked.

"Sure, I guess."

"Then it's a promise." Amy felt a surge of triumph. Every conversation Amy had with Beatrice that didn't end with the girl running away sobbing, felt like a victory.

Their conversation lulled as they watched Tim splashing in the shallows with the younger children. Amy stood, brushing off her skirt. "Come on, let's join them. The water's too inviting to resist."

"All right." Beatrice's reply was still guarded, but she rose to her feet.

Together, they waded into the cool embrace of the creek. Tim glanced over, a wide grin spreading across his face as he saw Beatrice approach. "Hey there, Beatrice! Ready to make a splash?"

"Maybe," she replied.

"Look out!" Tim scooped up a handful of water and playfully tossed it toward them, eliciting delighted shrieks from the children.

Amy laughed, the sound light and free as the droplets landed on her skin. She caught Beatrice's eye, sharing a conspiratorial glance before they both plunged into the water, splashing and laughing alongside the others.

Amy took her turn, swinging the little ones into the air before letting them plop back into the water, each child's laughter mixing with the next until it was impossible to tell one giggle from another.

Tim's voice rang out above the din, "Careful now, don't go turning the creek into a stormy sea!"

"Too late, Pa!" George called back, swimming past.

Amy dusted off her hands, a secretive twinkle in her eye as she reached into the picnic basket that had been carefully positioned in the shade. "I have one more surprise," she announced, her voice tinged with excitement.

"More food?" George's eyes widened comically as Amy pulled out a tin wrapped in a red and white checkered cloth.

"Thought we could use a little sweetness to end our day," she said, opening the tin to reveal an array of golden-brown treats.

"Yay!" George exclaimed, snatching a cookie and biting into it with gusto. His eyes closed in bliss. "Amy, you have to promise me something," he said after swallowing the delicious mouthful. "Promise you'll never leave. I don't think I'd survive without your cooking."

Amy laughed and handed out cookies to each eager hand. "I think I can promise that, George."

Amy helped gather the remnants of their picnic. She folded the blanket with care, musing over the laughter shared and the barriers broken down, especially with Beatrice.

"Thanks for today, Amy," Beatrice murmured, almost shyly, as they walked back to the ranch.

"Anytime, Beatrice," Amy replied warmly, feeling a deep sense of belonging. She looked back at the creek, her heart full. Every memory they made brought them all closer together.

THE RANCH HOUSE GLOWED with a warm light as dusk settled over the prairie. Inside, Amy read from a book of fairy tales.

"And they lived happily ever after," she finished, closing the book with a gentle thud. The children, nestled in their beds, looked up at her with sleepy eyes, the adventures of princes and princesses dancing in their heads.

"Goodnight," Amy whispered, leaning down to press a kiss on each forehead.

"Night, Amy," they murmured back, their voices a chorus of contentment.

Tim stood in the doorway, a tender smile playing on his lips as he watched Amy tuck the little ones in. He stepped forward when she was done, adding his own goodnight wishes. "Sleep tight, don't let the bedbugs bite," he said, ruffling George's hair.

"Only if Amy keeps making those cookies," George replied with a yawn, heading for his own room.

Amy chuckled softly, her heart swelling with love for these children who had become her own. She followed Tim out of the room, flicking off the light and closing the door behind them with a quiet click.

In the sanctuary of their bedroom, Amy snuggled into Tim's embrace, resting her head against his chest. "I always dreamt of this," she confessed. "A home, a family...it's more than I ever hoped for."

Tim tightened his hold, his chin resting atop her head. "You've brought life back to this place, Amy. To us." His voice was gruff with emotion. "I don't know how we managed before you."

She tilted her face up to meet his gaze, her eyes shining. "Together, we're stronger," she said simply.

"Stronger and happier," he agreed, bending to capture her lips with his own in a kiss that held promises of forever.

As they lay there, entwined in each other's arms, Amy knew she had found her place in the world. And Tim, feeling the beat of her heart against his, knew he had found his saving grace.

Chapter Eleven

Amy's eyes flickered open in the pitch darkness, a wave of heat washing over her. Her nightgown clung to her damp skin as she shivered beneath the quilts. With a weak hand, she shook Tim's shoulder, her voice but a hoarse whisper. "Tim...I feel awful."

Tim stirred. "What is it?" he murmured as he reached for the matches on the bedside table.

"Feels like I'm burning up," Amy said, trying to sit up but managing only to prop herself against the pillows.

With swift movements, Tim struck a match and the lamp flickered to life. He leaned in close, pressing the back of his hand to Amy's forehead. "You're burning up" he noted with concern etched into his brow.

"Please, can you get Brenda?" Amy asked. Brenda could be prickly as a cactus, but her adeptness with ailments was impressive.

"Of course, sweetheart." Tim kissed her forehead, already moving to pull on his boots. "Just lie back and rest. I'll be back as quick as I can."

Amy watched Tim stride through the doorway before sinking back onto the pillows. She trusted him implicitly, and she was pleased he was taking her illness—whatever it was—seriously.

Tim ran the entire way to Brenda's house. Moonlight draped over the rolling fields, guiding him to the porch where he didn't bother with a polite knock.

"Brenda!" His voice was urgent(he sends her husband for the doctor). The door creaked open, and a sleepy-eyed Brenda appeared, a shawl wrapped around her shoulders.

"Tim? What's wrong?" Her voice was sharp with sleep but edged with concern.

"It's Amy," he said, catching his breath. "She's got a terrible fever."

Brenda's eyes snapped fully open,. "I'm coming." She turned back into the house, calling over her shoulder, "Get Seth to ride for Doc Stanton!"

"Already planning on it," Tim answered, nodding as he saw Seth, bare-chested with suspenders hanging loose, grab his hat and stride out the door toward the stables.

"Let's go," Brenda said, now with boots laced and determination set in her brow.

Inside the ranch house, Amy tried to keep her mind on happier things — the scent of fresh bread in the oven, the laughter of children playing. But worry crept in like unwelcome shadows. Her breathing came in shallow bursts as she clutched the quilt tighter, her body slick with sweat.

"Come on, Amy, stay strong," she whispered to herself. Her thoughts wandered to the garden she nurtured, the comfort of the kitchen, the joy of feeding those she loved. They needed her, and she wouldn't let them down.

"Tim will be back soon," she murmured, the sound of her voice a small comfort in the dim room. "And Brenda...Brenda never lets anything beat her." She clutched a hand to her chest as a wave of deep, heavy coughing racked her body.

She closed her eyes, envisioning the hearty meals she'd cook once this fever passed, the cakes she'd bake, and the smiles they'd bring. With each image, her breathing steadied, the warmth of imagined ovens fighting the chill that had nothing to do with the night air. She was supposed to start on Beatrice's dresses tomorrow. The girl would be so disappointed.

"Family," she breathed out. Her family would see her through.

Tim burst through the bedroom door, the small medical kit in hand. He set it down on the bedside table with a reassuring thud.

"Let's take a look at you," he said as he leaned over Amy to feel her forehead. She managed a weak smile, bolstered by his presence.

"Feels like a furnace in here," Brenda remarked. " Why are you sick? You're never sick! Only you would get sick in the middle of the night with a whole family counting on you. You're burning up." Brenda shook her head.

"Could be anything out here," Tim mused, pulling a cloth from the kit and dampening it with cool water. "We'll figure it out, though." His hands were gentle as he placed the compress on Amy's forehead.

"Mrs. Jackson used to swear by this herbal concoction for fevers," Brenda said. "Might do the trick until Doc gets here."

"Sounds like something we should try," Tim said, standing up. "What did it have in it again?"

"Willow bark, I think...and some peppermint," Brenda replied, tucking a strand of Amy's hair behind her ear. "And wasn't there honey?"

"Yes, honey," Amy said, her voice weak.

"Right," Tim nodded, already moving toward the kitchen. "I'll whip it up. Keep her company for me?"

"Of course," Brenda answered, her voice soft as she took Amy's hand. "Remember when we all came down with the chickenpox? You made that oatmeal bath that had us all laughing 'cause we looked like breakfast."

Amy's lips quirked into a faint smile at the memory.

"Seems I'm always taking care of all of you," she whispered, her voice hoarse but tinged with warmth.

"Hey, it's our turn now. Don't you worry," Brenda reassured her. "Just focus on getting better. Imagine all those hungry mouths waiting for your food."

"Can't disappoint the children," Amy agreed.

"That's the spirit," Brenda said with a grin. "Now, let's get you fixed up so you can go back to bossing everyone around."

Tim returned with a steaming mug. "Here we go," he said, handing the remedy to Amy.

Amy's hands shook slightly as she took the mug. She sipped carefully, the sweet and minty concoction soothing her raw throat and warming her from the inside out. A sigh escaped her lips.

"Thank you, Tim," Amy said. "And Brenda, for being here."

"Family looks after family," Brenda chimed in, brushing a comforting hand across Amy's forehead. "It's no more than what you'd do for us."

"Very true," Tim added, pulling up a chair beside the bed. "You rest now. We're right here."

The night stretched on, a silent sentinel over the isolated ranch. Tim and Brenda settled into a rhythm, one watching Amy while the other (it's June in Texas so I doubt they needed a fire) fetched fresh water for her to drink. They spoke in hushed tones, snippets of stories from their childhood together spilling into the quiet room.

"Remember when we tried to bake that apple pie?" Brenda asked. "I thought for sure we'd burnt down the kitchen."

"And yet," Amy rasped, a faint chuckle accompanying her words, "it was the best-tasting charcoal we ever did eat."

"Your pies are much better now," Tim said, enjoying the story immensely. "Children'll be missing those if you don't get well soon."

"I can't let them down," said Amy, determination threading through her weakening voice. They'd already lost their mother. They didn't need to lose a second person in their lives.

"Of course not," Brenda reassured her. "You're too stubborn to let a little fever keep you from your duties."

"Stubborn and caring," Tim added, his tone affectionate. "A mighty combination."

As dawn broke, Amy's fever seemed to wane, the cool touch of Brenda's hand on her brow confirming it. The three of them were all relieved, but they needed the doctor to determine what was truly wrong.

"Looks like you're turning the corner," Tim observed, pouring Amy another cup of water.

"Thanks to you both," Amy said, her voice stronger now. "I don't know what I'd do without you."

"Let's not find out," Brenda replied, her bluntness softened by the warmth in her eyes. "Now, how about trying to get some more sleep?"

"Best idea I've heard all night," Amy agreed, closing her eyes and sinking deeper into her pillows, surrounded by the love and care of her dearest companions.

The latch clicked and the door creaked open, letting in a sliver of daylight that cut through the dimness of the room. Dr. Stanton stepped inside, his bag of instruments in hand, his face etched with concern. Tim hovered in the background as the doctor approached Amy's bedside.

"Morning, Amy," the doctor greeted, his voice a low rumble. He leaned over her, his hands practiced and efficient as he checked her pulse and listened to her breathing.

"Feels like fire's been burning through my bones," Amy said weakly.

"Let's have a look then," Dr. Stanton murmured, peering into her eyes, then down her throat. After a few moments, he straightened up, his brows knitted together. "Symptoms are worrisome. Could be Tuberculosis."

Tim's heart clenched at the word, and he exchanged a worried glance with Brenda who stood rigid, her hands clasped tightly.

"Is it...?" Brenda began, but her voice trailed off.

"Can't say for certain," the doctor continued. "For now, rest and take these medicines." He laid out bottles on the nightstand. "Keep her hydrated and isolated from the children."

"Of course, Doctor," Tim assured him, determination setting his jaw. "We'll do whatever it takes." He wasn't sure what they would do if she didn't get better. Beatrice was just warming up to Amy, and he was sure the girl would lose her mind if they lost her.

"Good man," said the doctor, tipping his hat to Brenda before making his way out.

An hour later, Amy's fever seemed to be gone entirely. "Look at you, fighting back," Brenda said, a smile breaking through her usually stern demeanor.

"Seems I've baked hotter things than this fever," Amy joked, her voice still frail but laced with her usual spunk.

"Your strength is showing," Tim chimed in, relief washing over him as he took Amy's hand gently. "You're one tough cookie."

"Cookie," Amy chuckled, the sound weak but genuine. "I could go for one of those."

"First thing you'll bake when you're up," Brenda promised her sassy tone back in play.

"Sounds good," Amy agreed, her eyelids fluttering with fatigue but her spirit undeniably brighter.

"Rest now," Tim said softly. "We got this, Amy. You just focus on getting better."

"Thank you," she whispered, allowing sleep to claim her once more.

TIM MOVED QUIETLY AROUND the kitchen, the early morning light casting soft shadows on the wooden countertops. He was no cook, not like Amy, but he could manage a simple breakfast. Oatmeal simmered in a pot, and he sliced a ripe peach to add some sweetness to it.

"Breakfast is almost ready," Tim called over his shoulder, not sure which of the children had joined him in the kitchen.

Beatrice frowned. "Why are you cooking? Where's Amy? We're supposed to make my dress today."

Tim shook his head. "Amy's sick, and the doctor fears it may be tuberculosis. It's going to be your job to keep the girls out of our bedroom. I worry this will last a while, and I can't deal with more than one sick person at a time."

She opened her eyes wide, and he knew Beatrice was afraid for Amy. "Is she going to die?"

"We won't know for a while. She's fighting hard, and the doc isn't sure that's what it is, but we're going to find out. Doctor is coming back this afternoon to check on her." He squeezed Beatrice's shoulder. "I'm going to take her some breakfast. You stay here."

He knocked softly on the bedroom door before opening it with the bowl of oatmeal in his hand. "Nothing fancy, just something to keep your strength up." Tim carried the bowl carefully to her bedside. "We need to talk about what's next for you."

Amy accepted the bowl with a small nod, cradling it in her hands. "I don't want any more fuss," she said after a spoonful

"Stubborn as ever," he remarked with a fond smile. "But we can't take chances with your health."

"More medicine?" she asked, her brow knotting with concern.

"Maybe. Dr. Stanton is going to take another look at you. Just to be sure."

Amy nodded, then sighed. "All right, Tim. If you think it's best."

"I am going to need to milk the cows and gather eggs. I've told Beatrice to keep the little girls out, and Brenda is still here." Tim's hand lingered on hers.

"Thank you," she whispered, a grateful smile touching her lips as she took another spoonful of oatmeal, the loving care of her family shining through even in the simplest of gestures.

As the day wore on, Tim continued working but checking on Amy every chance he got. Brenda perched at her bedside. The gentle brush of a cool cloth across Amy's forehead was soothing, as Brenda hummed an old tune, the notes dancing lightly around the room.

"Can't say I find much joy in the kitchen," Brenda quipped with a smirk, "but I'd bake you a hundred pies if it'd make you better faster."

Amy chuckled weakly. "I'd get better faster if you could cook lunch and supper. From what I've heard, Tim isn't much of a cook," she said.

"Rest now," Brenda said. "I'll feed them. No need for them catching what you've got."

"Miss their laughter," Amy said.

"Laughter will fill these walls again soon enough," Brenda assured her, squeezing her hand gently.

Hours passed, the room filled with nothing but shared silence and the rustle of pages as Brenda read from a well-worn book.

The creak of the door signaled Tim's return, his boots tapping a steady rhythm on the wooden floor. Behind him, Dr. Stanton, his bag in hand, offered a nod of greeting. Amy watched as they approached.

"Good news," Dr. Stanton said softly. "It's only bronchitis, which doesn't compare to Tuberculosis. You're going to be fine."

"Bronchitis?" Amy repeated, the word foreign yet somehow less frightening than the alternatives.

"Yes," the doctor confirmed, stowing his stethoscope. "Keep up with the remedies. They seem to be doing the trick."

A wave of relief washed over Amy, leaving behind a sense of hope as warm and comforting as the morning sun. "Thank you, both of you," she said, finding strength in their presence.

"Nothing to thank us for," Tim replied. "You're my wife, and I need you healthy."

"Get some rest," Brenda said, standing to stretch. "You'll need your strength for all those pies you'll be baking."

"But you're cooking tonight," Amy settled back against the pillows.

Brenda made a face as she nodded. "I'll cook supper."

BEATRICE APPROACHED Brenda in the kitchen. "Where's Amy?"

Brenda frowned. "Didn't your father tell you she was sick?"

"Too sick to cook?" Beatrice asked, looking belligerent.

"For a while, yes. But she will get better. At least the doctor says she will."

"Can I take her supper to her?" Beatrice asked.

Brenda shook her head. "No, we're still keeping you away from her. She'll be back to cooking soon."

Beatrice sighed. "I want to help her."

"Then let's make supper together! That's a way you can help."

"I guess..."

Beatrice followed Brenda's instructions on what to do and thought about how much she preferred cooking with Amy. She was ready for her to be well again.

Chapter Twelve

Timothy's weary eyes fluttered open. The dull ache in his bones was a testament to the back-breaking work that awaited him, as regular as the dawn. He sat up in bed, running a hand through his hair, and allowed himself a solitary moment to acknowledge the weight settling on his shoulders.

With practiced movements, Tim swung his legs over the bed's edge. He dressed swiftly in the dim light, pulling on his faded jeans and a shirt that had seen better days. Laundry really needed to be done, but short of asking Brenda for more than he already had, it wasn't going to get done. It was all he could do to keep up with his ranch chores, cook breakfast, convince the kids that Amy was all right, and make sure she ate and took her medicine. He'd had no idea what a strain being a caregiver put on someone. Thankfully, Felicity's mother had been visiting when she took ill, and she'd taken care of her daughter and grandchildren.

He stepped outside, feeling the heat and humidity burrow its way inside him. He often thought he should move to somewhere like Montana to ranch, but it was too cold in the winter there. There was no winning where temperature was concerned.

"Morning, old girl," he greeted the chestnut mare tied near the barn, her coat gleaming in the new light.

Tim scooped feed into troughs, his hands moving with the efficiency borne of countless mornings just like this one. His muscles remembered the routine, even if his mind was elsewhere.

"Pa, you fix that fence by the creek yet?" George called out, emerging from the tool shed with a hammer in hand.

"Planning on it after I fix breakfast," Tim replied, wiping sweat from his brow with the back of his hand. "You want to give me a hand?"

"Sure thing, Pa," George said. He was growing up fast, eager to walk in his father's boots, and Tim couldn't help but feel a surge of paternal pride.

As soon as they'd finished breakfast, leaving the dishes for Brenda, they walked the length of the pasture, inspecting the barbed wire. They worked in silent agreement, Tim showing George the ropes while fixing the loose strands that threatened the boundary of their land.

"Looks good, son," Tim nodded, satisfied with their handiwork. "Keep this up, and you'll be running your own place in no time."

"Hope so," George grinned, the image of youthful optimism.

Tim heaved another bale of hay onto the wagon, his muscles protesting as much as his mind. He paused, leaning against the wagon's edge, feeling the rough wood grain press into his palms.

"Pa, you all right?" asked George, his brow furrowed with concern.

"Ah, just thinking," Tim replied. His gaze drifted toward the house where Amy lay ill, her nurturing presence sorely missed in every corner of their home.

"Amy's going to be fine, Pa," George added.

"Sure, son," Tim said, though the knot in his stomach tightened. "Let's get back to work."

As the day wore on, chipping away at the endless list of chores, Tim's thoughts were never far from Amy. The livestock fed and watered, fences mended, and yet an important piece was missing.

Stepping inside the sweltering heat of the house, Tim found Amy propped up in bed, a shawl wrapped around her thin shoulders. Her breaths came shallow and labored, the sound like rustling dry leaves. She offered him a weak smile, and it struck him how something as simple as breathing could become such an arduous task.

"Hey there," he muttered, taking a seat beside her. His large hands felt clumsy as he touched her forehead.

"Tim..." she whispered, her voice barely audible, "the children..."

"They're fine, Amy. Focus on getting better, all right?"

The lines on Tim's face deepened with worry as he watched her struggle for each breath. He knew the ranch demanded his attention, but the thought of leaving her side, even for a moment, twisted his heart with guilt.

"Get some rest, Amy. I'll be right outside if you need me," Tim assured her, brushing a stray lock of hair from her forehead.

Leaving their room, he closed the door gently behind him. Outside, the ranch sprawled before him, its needs vast and unending. But within those walls, Amy fought a battle that dwarfed all others.

"Pa?" George's voice called from the porch.

"Coming, son," Tim answered, squaring his shoulders. If the ranch was his legacy, Amy and his children were his lifeblood. And he would find a way to nurture both, no matter the cost.

"PA?" GEORGE'S VOICE called again from outside, urgency lacing the word.

"Coming, son! Just give me a second!" Tim raised his voice in response, then immediately regretted it. He turned back to Amy, his features softening. "I gotta go see what he needs. Will you be all right for a spell?"

"Go," she insisted, managing a nod. "The ranch won't run itself."

He lingered for a heartbeat longer. With a reluctant sigh, he brushed a kiss on her forehead and stood. As he stepped toward the door, Amy's voice stopped him.

"Tim?"

"Yeah?" He turned, hope flickering in his chest for reconciliation.

"Could you leave the door open? Just a little. So, I can at least hear the girls?"

"Of course," he said, leaving a slice of daylight breaking into the room. It was a small comfort, but if it helped Amy feel less isolated, he was all for it.

"PA, WE NEED MORE WIRE for the fence," George called out. The boy stood by the paddock with a concerned furrow etched into his brow.

"All right," Tim replied, trying to keep the weariness from seeping into his voice. "I'll head into town later and pick some up."

"Don't you need to give Amy her medicine?" George asked, hesitant.

"Right." The word came out like a sigh. Tim's hand found its way to his hat, lifting it off to run a hand through his hair in frustration. The cattle needed tending, the fences repair, and Amy—his heart clenched at the thought—Amy needed him more than ever.

"Maybe Amy's friend Cassandra can help," George suggested tentatively.

"Maybe." Tim replaced his hat and nodded.

"MORNING, TIM," CASSANDRA greeted with a smile as she wiped her hands on her apron. "You're here awfully early."

"Morning, Cassandra," Tim nodded.

"Sit down, Tim. You look like you've been wrangling thunderstorms instead of cattle," Andrew, Cassandra's husband, said.

"Feels about right," Tim admitted. "It's Amy...she's got bronchitis, and I'm trying to keep the ranch from falling apart."

Cassandra shook her head. "You should have let us know sooner! I'll gather our other 'sisters' and we'll come over."

"Brenda's already been helping," Tim said. "I'm surprised at how much Amy does every day, and I didn't appreciate it much when she was healthy."

Cassandra sighed. "Amy's always been that way. Hurry home, and I'll get it all organized for you. Stop worrying."

Andrew nodded. "I'll talk to the others. I would bet David has a couple of hands he can loan you for a bit. His boys'll pick up the slack."

ENTERING THE BEDROOM where Amy rested, Tim found her propped up against pillows, her cheeks flushed from fever, yet there was a determined glint in her tired eyes. Tim took a seat beside her, taking her hand gently in his.

"I've been going crazy trying to manage this ranch and caring for you."

Amy offered a weak smile. "You're doing your best, Tim."

"Best ain't good enough," he countered softly. "I've been blind, Amy. Blind to what's truly important." He squeezed her hand, feeling the delicate bones beneath her skin. "From now on, you come first. I'll find a way to keep everything running, but not at the expense of us."

Her eyes shone with unshed tears. "Tim, I don't want to keep you from doing all you can for the ranch."

"Shush now," Tim interrupted gently. "You aren't holding me back. You're the reason I push forward. I've spoken to Cassandra and Andrew, and they reminded me we got a whole church ready to lend a hand. Cassandra is gathering all your sisters to help."

"Really?" A hopeful note entered her voice.

"Really. We're going to get through this together, Amy. You, me, the kids, and our neighbors. Like one big family." His thumb caressed the back of her hand.

Amy nodded, her spirit rallying.

"Promise me something, Amy. Promise me you'll focus on getting better. Let me worry about the rest."

"I promise, Tim," she said, her voice stronger than before. "And I'll bake you an apple pie as soon as I'm up and about."

"You will not hear me complain about that!"

AMY WOKE WITH A START. There was a lot of noise coming from outside her room, and she swung her legs out of bed. She walked to the bedroom door and peeked out. "Get back in bed!" Brenda said, putting her hands on her hips. "You've taken care of every one of us while we were sick. Now we're going to return the favor. I'm going to keep watching over you. Cassandra is going to make the girls' dresses you promised them. Deb is going to do all the laundry including that filthy gown you're in. Erna's going to cook all the meals and bake sweets for the kids and Tim. Faith is going to be scrubbing floors and dusting. Gail is going to build that playhouse and not worry about you paying her back. Susan is going to cook in Gail's place. Hannah is making lace collars for Beatrice's dresses. And last, but never least, Imogene is going to water and weed your garden while Ruby and Priscilla help."

Amy blinked a few times as she allowed her friend to help her back in bed. "Now stay where I put you!" Brenda said.

"What's Beatrice doing?" Amy asked, hating she couldn't make dresses with the girl.

"She's helping with dress duty. And helping with the laundry," Brenda said. "She keeps asking to see you, and even though the doctor said it's probably safe, I don't want to risk it."

"I would never risk any of the children. Good call." Amy swung her legs back into the bed, feeling as if she'd just run across the ranch and into town. "Back to sleep with me." She lay down, closing her eyes. "And Brenda?"

"Yes?"

"Thank you! Hug all the sisters for me."

"Of course!" Brenda said, smiling as she closed the door behind her.

Chapter Thirteen

Amy stepped out into the hallway. It had been a long two weeks in bed, but now her strength was returning, and with it, a hunger for the life that bustled beyond her door.

"Amy, you're up!" Priscilla yelled.

"Are you feeling better?" Ruby asked.

"Is it safe for us to be close to you?" Beatrice asked.

Amy couldn't help but smile at the trio of worried faces before her. "Yes, I'm much better," she declared, her voice still weak.

In an instant, their collective relief manifested in a whirlwind hug. She laughed, wrapping her arms around the three girls.

"Let's go see what Brenda's whipped up for lunch," Amy suggested, her stomach reminding her of its neglected state.

"Look who's finally graced us with her presence," Brenda called over her shoulder, a teasing lilt to her words.

"Wouldn't miss your cooking for the world," Amy quipped, a playful jab at Brenda's well-known distaste for culinary duties.

"Ha! You'll eat anything after two weeks of invalid food," Brenda retorted, but her smile was warm as she plated a generous portion for Amy and smaller ones for the children. "Was going to bring this to your room, but I think sitting up will do you some good."

"Thank you, Brenda," Amy said, taking her seat at the table.

"Slow down now," Brenda chided gently, passing a basket of rolls. "No need to rush when you have all the time in the world to enjoy it."

"Can't help it," Amy replied, savoring a forkful of tender carrots. "It's just so nice to be here, with all of you."

"Where else would you be?" Brenda teased.

Amy looked around at the eager faces that filled the small kitchen. This was home, and she was right where she belonged.

The clatter of boots on the wooden floor announced Tim and George's arrival before they even crossed the threshold. Amy lifted her gaze from her plate, her eyes lighting up at the sight of the two as they strode into the kitchen.

"Amy!" George exclaimed with a grin that stretched from ear to ear. He rushed over to Amy, his hands held out as if he still couldn't believe she was there, sitting up and well.

Tim's face broke into a warm smile, his relief obvious as he followed behind his son. "Well, look at you, Amy," he said, his voice rich with affection. "Back at the heart of this house where you belong."

"Feels like forever since I've seen you here," George chimed in, pulling up a chair next to Amy. His eager eyes swept over the spread on the table, but he waited, his respect for Amy evident in his patient pause.

Amy chuckled softly, taking in the sight of them both. "It feels so good to be in the kitchen again," she assured, her voice still weak but full of resolve. She looked around the room. "Not a single speck of dirt anywhere. You've kept the place just perfect."

"Your sisters saved my sanity," Tim said, his voice tinged with humor. He reached for a roll, his movements easy and unhurried.

"Once I'm up to it," Amy continued, "I'll have all my sisters over for a big meal. It's been too long since we've all been together."

"Easy there," Tim cautioned gently. "You need to get your strength back first."

"Of course," Amy agreed with a nod. "But it's something to look forward to."

As Amy's gaze wandered from the warm faces around her, it landed on the wooden structure outside the window, perched in the boughs of an old oak. "Is that the treehouse?" she asked. She felt like she'd missed years of her family's lives and not just two weeks.

"Yes," Brenda said from across the table, "the girls have been dying to show you their dresses too."

"I can't wait to see," she said, though her body sagged slightly.

Brenda caught the subtle droop of Amy's shoulders and clucked her tongue. "You aren't strong enough yet! Give it time."

From the corner of her eye, Amy noticed George. The boy was watching her intently. His concern touched her deeply, but before she could offer words of reassurance, Tim's hearty laughter filled the room, drawing her attention.

"Your face, George!" Tim laughed, nudging his son gently. "You'd think Amy was a ghost the way you're staring."

George's cheeks flushed, but he smiled.

"Can't blame him," Amy joked. "It's been a spell since I've joined y'all like this."

"True enough," Tim said, still smiling.

The meal continued, and Amy was so happy to be able to be a part of it. But as the minutes ticked by, her energy waned, and soon, the simple act of keeping her eyes open became a battle. With gentle insistence from Brenda, Amy conceded, allowing herself to be helped back to bed.

The moment her head touched the pillow, fatigue threatened to pull her under, but Brenda's voice cut through the haze. "Now, don't you go falling asleep just yet," she warned, the door clicking shut behind her. "The girls and I have a surprise cooked up for you."

"Surprise?" Amy said, curiosity flickering. She propped herself against the pillows, determined to stay awake. The thought of what the girls had planned brought a fragile spark of anticipation to her chest, a soft glow in the quiet of her room.

Amy blinked back the heaviness in her eyelids as she sat upright, propped by a mound of pillows. She resisted the pull of sleep with every ounce of will she possessed. The murmurs and giggles from beyond the door piqued her curiosity.

"Stay awake, stay awake," she whispered to herself, a mantra to fend off the encroaching slumber.

The door creaked open, and a parade of excitement spilled into the room. One by one, the girls twirled in, each adorned in a new dress.

"Look, Amy!" Priscilla said, spinning so her skirts flared out like petals on a blooming flower. "It's pink!"

"And mine has lace! Hannah even taught me how to make lace myself!" Beatrice told her, her hands skimming over the delicate trim with reverence.

"Do you think it's as red as a ruby?" Ruby asked.

With each presentation, Amy clapped and praised, her fatigue all but forgotten amidst girls, gowns, and giggles. She saw how they basked in her attention—these girls who had become her daughters—and felt her heart swell with a love that was both fierce and tender.

"All of you look beautiful," Amy said.

"We love them," Priscilla said. "And we learned so much as Cassandra taught us to sew them."

"Missed you lots," Beatrice said warmly. Amy thought maybe, just maybe, she and Beatrice would be able to get along better now.

Amy eased herself back against the pillows. Life, with all its simple pleasures, felt whole again.

"Thank you all for showing me," she said.

A shadow fell across the quilt as Beatrice perched beside her. The girl, usually a tempest of bottled emotions, sat silent, watching Amy with an intensity that seemed to weigh her down.

"Beatrice?" Amy's brow creased with concern, catching a shimmer in the young girl's eye.

"I just..." Beatrice said, "I want to say something."

"Go on," Amy encouraged, curious about what stirred behind those troubled eyes.

Beatrice took a deep breath. "I'm really thankful for you, Amy," she confessed, "for coming to live with us." She fiddled with the edge of Amy's blanket, not meeting her gaze.

"You're...You're a wonderful Ma. Better than I ever thought we could have again."

Amy reached out, resting her hand over Beatrice's. Their fingers intertwined, bridging the gap of past misunderstandings.

"Thank you, Beatrice," Amy replied, her throat tightening with emotion.

"And I'm sorry," Beatrice continued, a lone tear slipping down her cheek, "for the way I've treated you. You've been nothing but kind."

"I have a feeling I'd have felt the same way you did if I'd lost my mother. Well, if I'd known my mother before losing her," Amy said.

Chapter Fourteen

Tim gently assisted Amy into the two-seat buggy. He climbed up beside her, taking the reins in his hands with practiced ease. The horse, familiar with the path, started at a leisurely pace, allowing them to look around at the beauty that surrounded them.

"Feels good to be out, doesn't it?" Tim asked, the corners of his mouth turning up in a gentle smile.

"Very," Amy agreed, her cheeks flushed with the faintest touch of color.

For a while, they rode in comfortable silence. As they passed the meadows that rolled like waves in the breeze, Tim cleared his throat, his voice growing solemn.

"Amy, I... " He paused, searching for the words. "When you were sick, my world had stopped spinning. I don't think I realized how much I...how much I cared for you until the thought of losing you became real."

Amy turned to look at him, her eyes wide with a mixture of surprise and something warmer, a spark of deep affection. "Tim, I never knew."

"Guess I didn't either, not really. Not until then," he admitted.

"Tim, I've always dreamed of having a big family," she confided. "But being here, with you and the children...For the first time, I feel like I'm part of something real, a true family."

After their drive, Tim and Amy sat out on the porch, side by side on the swing. Tim reached for Amy's hand, his fingers weaving through hers with an easy familiarity.

"Amy, I love you," he said softly.

"I love you too, Tim," she whispered back.

Later that night, as they were all getting ready for bed, Amy found herself in the little girls' room, a thick book of fairy tales propped open on her lap. The girls lay tucked into their beds. Amy's voice breathed life into the age-old stories of knights and dragons, princesses and magic spells.

Tim stood just outside the doorway, leaning against the frame. He watched Amy with a tender gaze, admiring the way her expressions changed with every twist and turn of the tale. Her love for storytelling and nurturing the fertile imaginations of their little ones was just another thread in the tapestry of her kindness.

"Goodnight," Amy said as the story came to an end, closing the book with a soft thud. The girls murmured their goodnights, and they closed their eyes.

Amy tiptoed around the room, tucking in both girls with care. She bent over their small beds, placing a gentle kiss on both foreheads. "Goodnight," she whispered.

"Goodnight, Amy," they echoed, their voices drowsy and content.

When she went to the next room, she kissed Beatrice goodnight and heard something unexpected. Beatrice looked up at Amy. There was a softness there that hadn't been before. "I love you too," she murmured, her voice barely above a whisper.

Amy's breath hitched, tears pricking at the corners of her eyes. She leaned down to hug Beatrice. "Sweet dreams, Beatrice."

George was next, and he smiled at her kiss and words of love. "Love you too, Amy."

Amy found her way back to her bedroom, where Tim awaited. His presence was a balm to her soul, his smile the kind that set her world right again.

Tim stepped forward and wrapped his arms around her, his embrace enveloping her in warmth and safety. "Amy, I think we're the luckiest people on God's green earth," he said.

She nestled into him, feeling the truth of his words resonate within her. "It feels like a dream, Tim. One I never want to wake from."

"God knew, Amy. He knew exactly what He was doing when He brought you to me." Tim's voice was filled with conviction, and he pulled back just enough to look into her eyes.

Amy gazed up into those eyes and nodded. "He did, didn't He?" Her voice trembled with the weight of her gratitude.

Tim nodded. "I couldn't believe I would ever find love again after Felicity. And look at me? Happy as a lark!"

Epilogue

Amy rocked gently on the swing, her hands resting atop the gentle swell of her belly. A smile played on her lips as she watched the two boys she'd brought into the world chase each other through the yard, their laughter rising to meet the chirping birds overhead.

"Look at them go," Tim said, his hands lightly massaging Amy's shoulders from where he sat behind her.

"Like two little whirlwinds," Amy replied. She tilted her head back to gaze up into Tim's eyes. "I always dreamed of this, you know? A family...laughter and love filling the air."

Tim bent down, planting a tender kiss atop her head. "And now it's all real." As they watched, Ruby and Priscilla hurried over to their twin brothers, Jake and Luke. They helped them up and then invited them to play hide and seek, a game the twins had barely mastered.

"Thanks to you." Her hand found his, giving it a gentle squeeze. "You made my dreams come true, Tim."

"Sweetheart, we made them come true together." His thumb brushed a reassuring rhythm against her skin. "It's us, Amy. Always has been."

The porch swing creaked under their combined weight, a comforting, familiar sound that underscored their conversation. Life had blossomed around them, simple yet full, in the heart of the home they built together. And as the shadows lengthened with the setting sun, Amy and Tim remained, wrapped in the quiet joy of their madhouse in the middle of their own little world.

Milton Keynes UK
Ingram Content Group UK Ltd.
UKHW050757220624
444380UK00001B/53